MOONBAY

short stories by ty pak

Library of Congress Catalog Card Number:
98-094005
ISBN 0-9667458-1-7

Moonbay, a collection of stories, by Ty Pak
1. "The Tiger Cub" originally appeared in
Amerasia Journal 18:3 (1992), 51-60.
2. "A Debt" originally appeared in The Literary
Realm 2 (1988), 236-244.
3. "Contrition" originally appeared in The Echo 1
(July 1987), 123-147.
4. "The Court Interpreter" originally appeared in
The Literary Realm (1993), 125-145.
5. "Moonbay" originally appeared in The Echo 2
(1988), 283-309.
6. "The Foe" originally appeared in the Hawaii
Review 15 (1984), 25-28.
7. "The Gardener" originally appeared in Bamboo
Ridge 21 (Winter 1983), 49-64.

The Woodhouse, Inc.
69 Bank St. #103
New York, NY 10014
(212) 741-6637

CONTENTS

The Tiger Cub   1

A Debt   25

Contrition   41

The Court Interpreter   89

Moonbay   121

The Foe   171

The Gardener   183

THE TIGER CUB

I went to pick up Young at the church about 10 p.m., when the meeting sponsored by her Women's Group would be over. The night's speaker had been some Korean American female sociologist from Stanford speaking on the integrational problems of Korean War orphans adopted by American families. The parking lot was still full and I had to park on the street two blocks away. The Fellowship Hall was abuzz with the babble and laughter of a few hundred women. Young was busy with the aftermath of an apparently successful evening. I positioned myself next to the table laden with sliced persimmons and other goodies, but it was just my luck to be near Minja Hong, the group's treasurer, who could not rest unless everybody in her radius joined in a circle.

"Mr. Pak!" she screamed. "Meet our guest speaker, Dr. Helen Strawson. Dr. Strawson, he is our president's husband."

I was obliged to turn and greet the personage in question, a few years younger than Young, bold eyes, round-faced, dimpled.

"Glad to meet you," she said in good Korean with no hint of American accent. "Your wife is a terrific organizer."

I mumbled something in reply, but mostly stared at her, overwhelmed by the uncanny impression that I had seen her somewhere. Where was it? Minja came to my rescue, pulling her prize away to other points of circular connection.

On the way home Young bubbled over with praise for Helen Strawson, while I drove, unlistening, preoccupied with the puzzle of her previous acquaintance.

"She was adopted herself. There are thousands of them like her all over the country, mostly one hundred percent Americanized. But she has kept her Korean identity intact and is now heading this crusade to reawaken their Korean consciousness and heritage, organizing a national conference, mailing list, journal,..."

Then it all came back: she was the Tiger Cub, the dimpled girl who had moved in next door to the Hans' with her mother and three renegade People's Army soldiers toward the end of the first Communist occupation of Seoul over four decades ago when I was twelve.

During the last week of June, home from school until further notice due to the "national emergency" (North Korea had attacked on Sunday, June 25, 1950) we heard the distant rumble of artillery fire in the north, which grew steadily louder. Huddled under the eaves out of the drizzle, some of us pretended to be experts at telling the bursts of artillery apart as friendly or hostile, though to my ear they all sounded the same. We commented on the refugees who trudged past the village in groups of ten or twenty, then hundreds, wet, mud-spattered, a sorry lot chased out of their homes and fields with whatever they could grab, little suspecting how soon we would be joining their ranks ourselves. By late afternoon Thursday artillery shells whistled overhead on their way to targets in Seoul, throwing the whole village into panic. Any of them might fall short and blow us all up. Everybody began fleeing into the hills, thinking they would find safety among the rocks and trees. By nightfall not a soul was left in the village, and our family was the last to leave, carrying nothing but a bag of ground rice and bundles of clothes, new-born Jungsoog strapped on my mother's back and three-year-old Sooyong piggybacked on my father's. We were heading for a gap in the mountain ridge that would take us over to the other side. One shell landed about fifty feet away, sending rocks the size of a man's head flying past us.

"Follow the shells as they hit the ground," Father said, "because they won't land in the same spot twice."

But the shells kept falling helter-skelter, some behind us, some far to the side, not obligingly ahead in the direction we wanted to go. I fell, skinning my knee, but quickly got to my feet, forgetting the pain. The terrain became steep and rocky as we groped our way through the bush in the dark, wet and slippery, until we stumbled into the campus of a Buddhist temple under a huge perpendicular bluff, presumably safe from any projectile because none would bend in mid flight and fall straight down. We squeezed into a room, reeking with humanity. Snuggled in a corner by the door, Sooyong and I were lulled by the roar of artillery, more insistent than before, though muted by the rain, now grown torrential, and mesmerized by the tracers, orange, red, and blue, that crisscrossed the black sky visible through the cracks. Small arms fire chattered in between the boom of artillery and stutter of machine guns. Street fighting had erupted in the capital.

At daybreak we returned to our house, amazed that nothing had been stolen. The Syngman Rhee regime was gone and Ilsung Kim's portraits hung everywhere alongside Stalin's with billboards announcing the new order of the day. Our family had just moved into the area because of its clean air and rustic surroundings and nobody in the village knew about us. The distance from Seoul as the crow flies wasn't much, as indeed it is now the hub of the northern sprawl of the metropolis, but then, forty-one years ago, cut off by the North

Mountains with Arirang Pass winding through Donam Valley as the only access, it was as out of place as Shangrila. Father needed a place like this on account of his bad lungs, which had forced him to sell his rubber shoe factory and ten-room mansion on Mali Heights. To prevent the Communists from finding out about him, a parttime English professor at Googmin University as well as a retired businessman, a reactionary by their standards, we gave out the story that he had gone to town and not returned. I did all the shopping and other errands that necessitated leaving the house. By and by the District People's Team came around and asked about Father. We stuck to the story we had agreed on.

"Tell him to report as soon as he returns to the District Office," they said. "Otherwise he would be arrested as an enemy of the people. We must all work together to defeat American imperialism and build a united fatherland."

We were grateful they didn't search the house. But he couldn't stay cooped up in the house forever. We had no food left and heard that rice could be gotten in exchange for clothes and other valuables at the farms across the river. Father set out early one morning with a bundle and returned late at night with a bag of rice he could barely carry. Though exhausted, he was exhilarated by the success of his mission. But, with many mouths to feed, the rice did not last long and Father had to leave again. This time he did not return at night, nor the next day or after. He was really missing now. Mother was going out of her mind and went to the District Office and everywhere else to look for him, though her movements were severely restricted by the total absence of public transportation and round-the-clock Allied air raids. Neighbors came and offered their various opinions, the dominant one being that he must have been picked up at one of the street checkpoints and drafted into the Voluntary Army, formed with conscripts from the occupied south. He was over forty and had tuberculosis and flaming hemorrhoids but that did not matter to the People's Army, eager to find fillers for their thinning ranks as they plowed deeper into the south, running into stiffer resistance from the US-led United Nations Command.

In the middle of the night one night he returned, his head bandaged. On the way home from his rice mission he had been waylaid by a communist cadre and pressed into the construction of a pontoon bridge across the river. He had to haul huge logs with other stronger men and got kicked and beaten for not pulling his weight. During an air raid he tried to escape but was pursued by a foreman who knocked him out with a blow of a stick on his head. As soon as he came to hours later, he had to go back to work, though his head throbbed and his vision blurred: otherwise they would have beaten him dead. One night there was a big air raid: a squadron of jets blew up all their days of work to smithereens. Everybody ran for shelter from the exploding bombs and machine gun bullets but Father was too weak to run. The air raid ceased but he was left alone. Nobody came around for hours. Slowly he made his way back home, dodging checkpoints.

"I have an awful headache," he said, collapsing to the floor.

Mother spread out the bedroll, heated up water, and gave him acorn bread on which we had been living: I had been going to the back hills with other villagers to pick the wild acorns, edible when their bitterness got bled out by soaking in water for a few days.

House to house search had begun for men of all ages. Our house seemed particularly vulnerable, as it was next to the Hans. Sangchun Han, who the villagers had thought to be a traveling salesman frequently absent from home, turned out to be a bigwig in the Communist regime. All through the summer months, ever since the Communist occupation began, the Hans' had been the focus of much traffic. The side of our house with the master bedroom and kitchen closed the mouth of their U-shaped building. Shades stopped our windows so we couldn't look into their interior but we could see pretty much of whatever went on there through the cracks. The rugged types that came and went, Party cadres, Youth League hit men, military brass, gave little comfort to the hiding man, as his coughs became more uncontrollable. He had to get away.

On his long health strolls Father used to hike all the way to a Buddhist temple a couple of miles up in the hills and had become acquainted with its abbot, to whom he applied for sanctuary. It was readily granted, with the understanding that whenever a search party was rumored or suspected of heading that way, Father was to hide himself in a cave further up the hill so as not to jeopardize the temple. It was my duty to bring him food, either to the temple or the cave. I have no idea how she did it, but Mother managed to get some food, probably by helping in the kitchen next door. I had to zigzag my way to the temple with the food, lest a communist soldier or party cadre should question me, though I had an answer prepared for that exigency.

The US Fifth Air Force flew their daily sorties of destruction and the sixteen-inch guns of the

Seventh Fleet, anchored offshore, pounded away, dumping so many tons of TNT per acre on Seoul. Saturation bombing, they called it. The city burned day and night, until nothing remained but rubble and cinder. To prevent the populace from getting accurate war news the Communists confiscated radios and prohibited listening on pain of instant execution. But we hid ours and listened, under a thick blanket. From these broadcasts we learned that MacArthur's Marines had landed at Inchon, but they seemed to take their time.

When I went up to the cave one day, Father complained of a wracking headache. I walked three miles to a pharmacist in Donamdong and, parting with the precious cash, bought twenty aspirin tablets. To my amazement he poured out and popped the whole lot into his mouth. That didn't bring him any relief. In fact, his headache grew worse.

"I want to go home this evening," Father said.

"What if they raid the house tonight?" I asked. "Mom says the Communists are carrying out last-minute roundups and reprisals."

"It makes no difference whether I die here or at home," he said, panting from the stabs of headache.

"Don't say such a thing, Dad. It will be over

soon."

"No, not this," he whispered, clutching his head in his hands.

I brought him home, practically carrying him the whole way.

Next morning we found the Hans' eerily quiet. It had been abandoned overnight. I wanted to go there and scrounge for food but Mother stopped me, saying it might be a trap.

Later that afternoon three Red soldiers entered the empty house with a woman in her early thirties and her daughter, four or five years old. Nobody could tell what their ranks were, whether they were officers or enlisted men. Going about in shirt sleeves and shorts, they broiled meat and drank wine, sang and danced, and carried on. The woman seemed to belong to all of them or to none, ministering to them all equally. They fawned on her without jealousy and took turns in playing with the child, piggybacking her, tossing or airplane-riding her. She giggled and screamed for joy. Air raids and naval bombardment might intensify and the Red Army be in disarray and retreat, but this little commune throve in blissful oblivion. Their merriment, continuing through the night, struck terror among those who waited for the American forces. Maybe MacArthur had never landed at Inchon. Maybe the Communists had never retreated. All these rumors about the collapse of the Red Army might be deliberate fabrications by the Communists themselves to separate friend from foe.

After lunching on acorn bread, I decided to have a look around outside. I couldn't hear the usual noise of neighborhood children playing in the square, of which our house and the Hans' formed one side. On the other side of the square, directly across from our gate, the Sohns operated a grocery store. Separated from them by a lane was the Pyos'. In his sixties and known for his erudition in classical Chinese, Mr. Pyo carried a cane, his young wife at his elbow. For days he never left his house. People said he had some dreadful disease, like cancer, but I couldn't believe it from his ruddy face, which was such a contrast to my father's pallor. A total of four lanes threaded through the closely-built houses and converged on the small square, barely half an acre wide, but the village children congregated and played there as if it were Disneyland.

With my rump I pushed the gate out and removed the latch from its cradle. As soon as the gate swung open inward with a loud squeak, a blond-haired American Marine put his M-1 to my chest, the sharp point of its bayonet digging into the skin. I spun around and fell flat on the ground, arms hugging my head. The wild pumping of my heart seemed to quiet down a little. Slowly I raised my head. Muzzle of his gun lowered, the blue-eyed American stood over me, watching, expressionless. Shamefaced, I rose, the American's muzzle following my every movement. Three Marines were on the roof, crouched behind the ridgeline and looking over into the Hans'. One of them, a Korean, motioned to me to move out of the house. Keeping myself in clear view of the watching American at the gate, I went to the door of the master bedroom, slid it open, and whispered to my parents that the Americans had arrived and we should all move out at once.

"We are delivered!" Mother exclaimed.

My subdued face muffled her jubilation. She and Sooyong stuck their heads out at the door and saw the American at the gate. I told them there were more on the roof and probably many more all around the house, ready to attack the Hans'. Sooyong shrank back, trembling and clinging to Mother's skirt, on the verge of tears. Comforting him she put him away and helped Father up, who flopped to the floor, knees buckling. I went in and gave her a hand in propping him up. She let go, so she could pick up Jungsoog. Father leaned his entire weight on me, but skin and bones, he was as light as a boy. Silently we made our way to the gate.

"You guys are here at last," Father said to the vigilant American in flawless English, taking him by surprise, who however only motioned us to the lane next to the grocery store where behind a squad of American Marines with a machine gun unit aimed at the Han gate crowded the villagers, rubbernecking and inching forward, tensely watching the unfolding drama. Other lanes were similarly guarded by marines with their own retinues of expectant spectators.

"Take me to the commanding officer!" Father asked.

It was like wanting to see MacArthur himself. Though embarrassed by his audacity I obeyed and led him to the command post by the Pyos'.

"You don't have to waste any fire power, Lieutenant," Father addressed the American officer with the gold bar. "They are all soundly asleep. They went to sleep after daybreak, after drinking and singing all night. Why don't you send in a few men, maybe over our roof or through one of our windows, and take them prisoner?"

"Risk the chance of killing my men?" said the American, turning to a Korean Marine interpreter who had come around to see what was up, as if Father had been talking through the interpreter all along. "No, we are storming the place right now."

"But that way you endanger your men more,

not to speak of property," Father persisted. "Go in our house and look for yourselves through a window and you'll see."

Father spoke with effort, beads of sweat on his upper lip, on his prematurely furrowed forehead.

"Tell him to get out of my way and mind his own business," said the American, again talking to the Korean Marine, who glared at Father.

A Sergeant on our roof watched for the Lieutenant's signal. The Lieutenant spoke to his Korean interpreter, who stood up and with another Korean Marine pushed back the villagers crowding forward beyond the forbidden line.

A hush fell on the whole village for a breathless second or two. Nothing stirred. The Lieutenant's hand rose and dipped. The Sergeant on the roof flung a satchel of grenades over the roof ridge into the Han courtyard. Automatic weapons, submachine guns and rifles opened up simultaneously. The grenades exploded. A black smoke spiraled up. Pieces of broken doors, furniture, roof tiles and glass fell in a shower over the square. A section of our eaves got blown off and the windows had shattered. From inside the Han house rose piercing screams above the crackle of firearms. The automatic weapons kept up their fierce bark. Two American Marines leaped to the left and right of a rupture in the front wall of the

14

besieged house, stuck their submachine guns in, and fired away wildly into the house, swinging the barrels.

Hugging her daughter, half dead with a split skull, the wounded woman, herself wounded in the face and bleeding, stumbled out through the wreckage of the smashed gate.

"Help, long live America," she bawled. "Long live the Republic of Korea. Help, long live, help,..."

An American Corporal flanking the gate pushed her with the point of his bayonet. She shrank with a muffled shriek. The Corporal jerked his chin, motioning her toward the command post. Crying, laughing, looking wildly about like a baited animal at the sea of hostile faces, she hobbled on.

"Help, long live the Republic of Korea, long live!" she went on like a broken record.

"Raise your hands, up, up," shouted the Americans at the gate to two men in their jocks limping out of the house, one supporting the other who was minus one leg from the knee. The supporting man was also hurt in the shoulder, blood rippling down his arm and chest. Obviously surprised in their sleep, they were dazed, still not fully comprehending their calamity.

In vain did the Marines try to get some information out of the shell-shocked, hysterical woman, who kept hugging her unconscious child protectively. The two male prisoners said their other friend was inside, fatally wounded with a piece of grenade lodged in his chest, a fact soon confirmed by a squad of Marines searching the house. The seized weapons, long shoulder rifles of Japanese make and some swords, were taken outside and shattered against a stone. Left in the pool of blood on the floor, neck twisted, limbs immobilized, upturned eyes fixed on a spot in the ceiling, the dying man groaned through the night and most of the next day. The cry began at a high pitch, then fell to a sob and puff. The pattern, rhythmic and regular, seemed set to go on forever. Gradually the moan became hoarse and weak, the intervals lengthened, sometimes for minutes. But just as we sighed thinking it was all over, we heard him again. Finally, all fell silent.

The villagers talked excitedly about the execution of the two soldiers and their whore. The bodies had been thrown into a ditch by the roadside near the main bridge. Anybody could go and look.

Meanwhile, Father became tongue-tied and unconscious. An Army medic came, took his pulse, and asked whether he had had any particular disease that we knew of. When we told him about his tuberculosis, the doctor nodded in confirmation and left hurriedly after leaving some cough drops. Father died a few days afterwards. With the months of malnutrition and tension Father's lungs must have become a sieve by then, but the immediate cause of his death, as indicated by the headache and locked tongue, was most probably subdural hematoma from the beating to his head, according to my brother Sooyong, an internist in La Palma, California. Without our knowing it his head had been literally bursting inside with the accumulation of blood.

In the grief and turmoil that followed Father's death I didn't have time to think about the inexplicable stragglers. In a few months the Red Chinese came to the aid of the North Koreans and Seoul had to be evacuated again. We had to leave joining the millions of dispossessed refugees. But even in the worst struggle to survive, go to school, and help the fatherless family as the eldest son, the enigma of the stragglers returned to baffle and disquiet me. I had seen many more deaths since, on the road, in the ditches, fields and hills, until I felt numb and immune to the sight. Certainly the anguish I had experienced upon losing my father had taken the sting out of any death. Nevertheless the death of the stragglers recurred to hound and needle me.

Nobody had paid attention to my father's suggestion that they might be taken prisoner more easily than by explosives. The village had needed a slaughter, a payment in blood, for all the months of hunger and frustration. The American liberators had to write their triumph in blood. I remembered feeling tense and worried when Father talked to the American Lieutenant. I actually resented him for meddling, for trying to deprive the villagers and me of the good show we deserved, and applauding the American's wisdom when he proceeded to give the signal. My mother felt the same way. Distraught with her husband's illness, she brightened up at the report of the Americans shooting all of them dead and dumping them in the ditch to rot. That was divine justice. She fumed upon learning that the Americans had come back to pick up the injured girl and taken her to the American hospital ship off Inchon. During her brief tenancy at the Hans' she had walked up and down the square looking in vain for playmates, her plump cheeks dimpled, her shapely lips pressed in defiance, her black, shining eyes fluttering with suspicion and anger. All the children in the neighborhood had shunned her.

"It's so unfair, so foolish," my mother had hissed. "Why didn't they leave her to die? It's like nursing a tiger cub, which is sure, as soon as it grows up, to turn back and bite the hand that has fed it. The Americans are making a big mistake.

Somebody ought to go and tell them."

She looked hopelessly at her delirious, tongue-tied husband. She was not alone in this sentiment. All the villagers resented the injustice of a Communist brat lying comfortably on an American bed, between clean white sheets, eating all the great food, getting the expensive medical care, while they starved and sickened.

Who were they, the stragglers? Why did they linger, instead of fleeing while they had the time? Were they cut off from the chain of command by incessant American bombing like the stranded pockets of Iraqis in the recent war? Could it have been some morbid hope that their lives might be spared, if they were taken prisoner? But their conduct had been hardly consistent with a program of surrender. Except for the woman, were they philosophers who despaired of any meaning or dignity in life and courted death, living it up for the remaining few days, hours, which could have been as tedious to them as they had been to us waiting for the arrival of the American Marines? The mystery had deepened with the years and oppressed me, an accomplice to the senseless, brutal, base massacre.

But I need no longer feel guilty on account of the Tiger Cub. They must have sewed her skull back together and some compassionate American doctor or nurse must have adopted her while she was still recuperating or some kindly family under the Foster Program later on as she grew up at an orphanage. She was the lucky one to have had all the education and advantage. Was Strawson her maiden or married name? In either case I had no doubt about her being my dimpled neighbor of a few days four decades ago. I could prove it by parting her hair and identifying the scar tissue that must crisscross her pate. But how was I, a married man, to go about proposing such familiarity without incurring the censure of immorality, nay, insanity?

Young was still going on with her rhapsody.

"Isn't she wonderful, a nationally known scholar in her field and yet so humble and genuine! There is nothing fake about her. She comes on straight and clean like a silver bell. It would have been so easy for a woman in her position to forget the Korean side of her identity entirely. She must be a role model for our children, for all Korean Americans. Incidentally, don't be shocked when you get the next statement from the bank: I have given her one thousand dollars for use in her work."

"You what!?" I exploded.

"As president I couldn't do any less. Besides it's tax deductible. It's a worthy cause. It's like giving the money to our own kids, investing in their future, to give them a sense of identity and self-respect,..."

I let her go on with her justification, acquiescing. Hadn't Mother foretold that the grown Tiger Cub would bite back? I was lucky to get away with that size bite, perhaps because I had no hand in her rearing.

A DEBT

For a while I didn't know whether I was alive or not. I couldn't move my limbs, torso, or neck. Does one go to limbo in rigor mortis? I wondered. Through a hole punched out before my eyes I could dimly make out the room. I was in a cast from head to foot. My left eye was bandaged over. Through my right eye I got only a cracked, blurred vision, as if from under water. The aches and sores all over my body synchronized for an excruciating orchestration of pain. Involuntarily, I let out a groan.

"Hi, you are awake, Lieutenant Park!" a man's voice said.

I struggled to speak but my lips seemed taped. Instinctively, I raised my hand to touch them, but only felt the fruitless tug at the solid wall of plaster. Concentrating on my tongue, I found it mobile. With a sigh of relief I pushed it out between the lips, wetting them at the same time. Inhaling and exhaling through the parted lips, I swished my tongue around in the mouth, tensing and laxing my vocal cords. It was like learning to speak all over again.

"Yes," I heard myself saying.

"Good," he said. "I am Dr. Swanson. Honored to treat a Distinguished Service Medalist. Here is the medal and letter of appreciation from the President of the U.S.A."

I tried hard to comprehend his effusion.

"Where am I?" I asked.

"Tripler Army Hospital in Honolulu," Dr. Swanson said.

"How long have I been here?"

"Two months. It's a miracle you've pulled through. There isn't a square inch of your body that is left whole. It's as if somebody had come between you and the bomb."

All of a sudden I remembered. We had been on the run all night long, caught in a Viet Cong ambush. In the confusion of bombs and screams, we had scattered beyond any hope of regrouping. Incongruously, through it all, George McDuff had stuck to me, tongue-tied like a mute, and was with me in the ditch dodging the ground-level barrage of machine gun fire that mowed the brush down. Then a grenade dropped only inches away. Before I could react George jumped up and threw his body on it.

"Yes, somebody has," I said.

"Of course I meant it as a figure of speech."

"No, it's the literal truth."

The doctor looked at me askance before breaking into an indulgent smile.

"You must be a Christian or something," he said.

I didn't know how to explain Private George McDuff to a stranger. Certainly nobody in my outfit would have expected him to do what he did to save me, a Korean, he had been programmed to look down on and antagonize. Was it an act of genuine sacrifice or some kind of temporary mental disorder? If it was the latter, wasn't I responsible? I did not intend or foresee any such permanent damage and meant only to teach him a lesson. He had practically driven me to it.

"Shut up, McDuff," I shouted, coming between him and Private Henry Eldrige, his reluctant audience. McDuff had been talking nonstop since we left the Brigade by armored personnel carrier. Dismounting at the end of the dirt road our 30-man patrol had started climbing in single file up the trail into the jungled valley of Lyuksam near the Laotian border, where a heavy concentration of Viet Cong regulars had been reported by the Army intelligence. McDuff wouldn't shut off.

"It's a free country, Lieutenant," he said defiantly.

"We are in Vietnam, in Viet Cong country," I said.

"An American is an American regardless of where he is. He is a free man and can't be muzzled like a Korean."

That was a deliberate dig at my nationality. Should I be provoked as he wanted me to be?

"That doesn't mean you can harm others," I said.

"I am doing nobody any harm, none that I can see."

"You think you are entertaining us?"

"Frankly yes. You should reward me for doing everything to lift up the morale of this droopy outfit."

"I don't see anybody laughing and dancing."

"Hey, Henry, do I bother you with my incessant conversation?"

Eldridge, a meek farm boy from Wisconsin, pretended as if he had not heard and kept walking a dozen feet ahead, eyes on the trail, barely visible through the overgrown grass, the favorite place for Viet Cong booby traps.

"Nobody is bleeding because of my talking, Lieutenant."

"Stop this nonsense at once."

"Nonsense, Lieutenant, when it makes the steps go lighter?"

"You think we are on a picnic?" I said, wondering at the unreality of this exchange. If anybody had told me six months ago that I as commanding officer would be going through this bizarre ritual of jawing with a private, I would have called him a nut. Nor was it a problem unique to my platoon due to my being an Asian, though with McDuff it definitely was a factor.

Discipline was not what it used to be and we had reports of officers getting killed doing a private's job because their men would not do what they were told. The whole nation, Pentagon, Congress, or whoever called the shots, seemed bent on subverting the Green Berets, the Army's elite corps. How else could they keep sending in replacements like McDuff for the many good men we lost?

Times were changing rapidly. A couple of years older than McDuff, I already felt like a hoary patriarch many generations older. I had come to Vietnam believing in our cause, in the purpose of our mission, to safeguard individual freedom and human dignity from the dictatorial forces that sought to enslave mankind. To fight and win ten thousand miles away from home meant protection of our own heritage, our own land and kin, Stars and Stripes, Statue of Liberty, hot dog and milk shake, everything we held dear and good. I had been unswerving in my convictions, in my patriotic fervor and martial zeal. But for months now we had been getting disturbing news from home. College campuses were in revolt and police had to go down and shoot. Even the professors, who should know better, had joined the students, demanding immediate cease-fire. Where did it leave us exactly, the fighting men in the field?

Robots or devils incarnate spreading destruction and genocide? Talk of taking the fight out of a fellow! Bewildered, motiveless, we went through the motions of fighting a war that drifted on directionless.

Maybe McDuff had been planted by the antiwar party to wreck the best fighting arm of the U.S. Army, though there wasn't much left to wreck. His records revealed no history of psychosis or abnormal behavior before or during bootcamp in the States. A white boy from Alabama with a graduate degree from Berkeley, he could have gone on to an officer training course or taken a civilian job that would have exempted him from the draft, but he had enlisted as a private instead. Could it be for anything but espionage and sabotage? Enervated, drained of will, I could not act even on such probability, and beheld the phenomenon of Private George McDuff with awe, as if he had been some new species.

I dismissed the possibility of his being a self-exiled romantic, turning to the Green Berets as the youth of Europe had in the olden days to the French Foreign Legion. Set in his ways, a slave to habit and prejudice, he lacked the detachment, resignation, indifference, characteristic of the disillusioned idealist. He was anything but indifferent or apathetic. I had no doubt he would have behaved differently if I had been an Anglo c.o., though under no circumstances he would have made a good soldier. Could a man's racial bigotry be so strong as to unhinge him? Most probably so, especially when coupled with the demon of fear.

McDuff could have gone through the hardship of Green Beret training in the States while it was just a matter of stamina and endurance, a workout for health, but upon arrival at the battlefield of Vietnam he could have been jolted into the chilling realization that he was in it for real, to kill or be killed swiftly, brutally by Viet Cong, small unglamorous Asiatic men and women, even children, using every weapon or dirty trick known to mankind. Yammering away might be one symptom of that awful naked gut-gripping fright which immobilizes a soldier before he faces a single live enemy with a rifle aimed at his breast. You lose this battle with yourself and you are finished as a fighting man. All your fine record as model driller at bootcamp or top student at the academy or war college counts for naught. You are nothing but dead weight that's going to pull your whole unit down to the ground. No, I wouldn't have that of any man fighting in my command, as long as we must fight on. Even in this kind of war, the fighting man owed it to his team to at least pull his weight, let alone display heroism. That was only fair. There was no room for sympathy with individual weakness or failure. In this department, thank God, McDuff made my job easy. I had absolutely no sympathy to spare for this jabbering racist.

"You may talk your head off for all I care," I said. "But you have no right to jeopardize the rest of us. You think you know everything."

"Not everything. Just enough to know my rights and keep my cool over nothing."

He was taunting and daring me. Did he know he had me over the barrel and could get away with it? No matter what he did or said I was not going to send him back to Personnel, which did not look favorably on any frontline commander sending an able-bodied recruit back as a reject instead of gratefully accepting him and making good use of him on whom, like the latest-model weapon, the Army had expended so many thousands of tax dollars. With careful screening, with emphasis on elitism in the case of the Green Berets. Impugn the wisdom of the whole intricate system of recruitment and training? I might as well call the Nobel laureates quacks and fakes. No, there was no sending him back once he had been assigned to me.

Being the only Korean c.o. in the whole brigade,

I stuck out like a sore thumb as it was. I didn't want to make my position any more conspicuous in the eyes of my superiors. The moment there was trouble, the first thing they would think of would be my ethnicity and the rationale of giving combat command to my race, rather than taking my word against the troublemaker, as in the case of a White officer. What rotten luck, how absolutely demeaning and dreary to be marked and handicapped by such an accident of birth as one's race! I may be a third-generation American, know the history and geography of my native land inside and out, be guaranteed equality under the Constitution, but felt penalized, castrated in subtle, invisible ways.

"I have a surprise for you yet," I swore inwardly. "I'll humble and break you, my dear Oriental-hater."

I did not yield to the pressure to send him back with a factual report on his conduct to date, which would guarantee his dishonorable discharge. In his distorted mind it might not count as dishonorable at all. Like O Henry's hobo who considers the county jail a free boarding house for his wintering purposes, McDuff might think he was ahead of the game for having earned his keep and other Green Beret benefits, including hazardous duty pay. No, the Army shall get its money's worth out of him yet, I had resolved. Repeatedly I had put off Sgt Richard Fuller, the man now at the head of our patrol, who wanted to pack him off to the Army shrinks, reassuring him that McDuff would shape up in time for combat.

"Don't you know the silence rule exists for good reason?" I said, sickened by McDuff's superior smile on his face. "You may give all of us away to the enemy."

"Look, Lieutenant. They can see us from miles around, right? Already their binoculars are trained on us, watching our every move. My voice range is only 100 feet, but their visual range is 10,000. So my speaking or not now has no bearing on our discovery. I thought Green Berets believed in getting things done, without getting hung up on stupid regulations like that."

With difficulty I suppressed an overwhelming desire to smack him across his grinning face, envying Major Yangshik Jo, the c.o. of a neighboring Korean contingent. A prick like McDuff would be straightened out in no time in the Korean Army. Everybody in my platoon might detest McDuff and consider him a menace to their own safety during combat if he kept up his garrulous penchant, but the moment I lifted a hand against him, I would never hear the end of it. The Korean placed above his station who lost his cool under stress.... The whole U.S. Congress would jump on my back. Besides I doubted whether hitting him would do him any good. Certainly not the humiliation of it. He had been humiliated enough - grounded for days, made to dig trenches, carry bazookas and equipment, run extra miles, for the offense, but nothing had registered. He simply had a compulsion to talk, seeking out his victims among those in his ambience.

"All right, wiseguy. Have it your own way. But once we are inside the jungle, I want you to button up, deader than a dead mouse. The Viet Cong are everywhere. I don't mind them sneaking up on you and slitting your throat but I mind that very much for anybody else."

As I hurried off so I could have the last word for a change, the idea came to me like a flash of lightning. I had hit on the very solution to shut him up once and for all.

It was pitch dark, like most nights in the Vietnam jungle. The platoon had camped on a huge slab of rock, skirted beneath by a stream. The pounding of a waterfall at some distance echoed in the meandering gully. Spaced a few feet apart from each other in an arc, sitting close to the edge of the cliff, every other man kept watch, taking turns with his sleeping buddy, the shifts averaging six overnight because few could stay awake much over an hour after a day of grueling march. McDuff was on the first watch. After a few minutes, perhaps bored or frightened, he started reciting the sutras in Sanskrit or something. That did it. I had no choice but to execute the extreme measure I had determined on.

It took nearly one hour to scale the overhanging rock, slipping and almost falling. The desperate handholds had held and the drone of the waterfall had drowned the noise of my clawing and flailing around. Undetected by any of my men and shuddering at the thought of me being a real Viet Cong, I came within striking distance of McDuff, still preoccupied with his audienceless recitation. What would a Viet Cong do next? At a bound, I threw an armlock around his throat, pinioned both his arms under my knees, and made an incision in his throat with my knife under the Adam's apple, avoiding the jugular.

Stunned, feeling the sharp edge and the spurt of blood, McDuff fainted, convinced that he had been killed. The commotion had awakened the whole platoon, as I slipped away unnoticed. It was hours before McDuff regained his senses after the medic had patched him up. Back at my post, I had the men standing by with a blanket to silence him in case he should start yelling his head off when he came to. But the anticipated hysteria did not materialize. Upon opening his eyes after daybreak, he looked from one man to another circled around him, his face ashen and expressionless, never uttering a word.

"Would you do me a favor, doctor?"

"Name it."

"Would you please arrange to send the balance of my savings account and the medal to the family of Private George McDuff, formerly with Charley Company, the 147th Brigade?"

"The medal, too?"

"Yes, he deserves it more than I."

"Well, it's yours, so I guess you can do whatever you want with it, but I've never heard of such a thing. He must have meant a lot to you."

"Yes," I said, closing the subject, knowing full well that I would always remain a debtor, no matter whether George knew what he was doing or not, that no gesture of munificence would make up for loss of life.

CONTRITION

"Are you sure she was on the plane?" asked John Minn.

"Yes. I've confirmed it with the KAL head office here," said Sam Char, his brother-in-law. "I have the printed passenger list in front of me."

"She may have changed her mind at the last minute," John said, not believing it himself.

"She did not cancel. She was on it. I drove her to the airport myself."

"Do they have anything new about the plane?"

"Not more than the first KAL announcement that the Soviet interceptors had forced it down."

John had heard it on the news, with no idea it would have anything to do with him.

"Did she take David with her?"

"No. He is here with us," Sam said.

Was there a hint of reproach in Sam's voice or was it his imagination? "Is he okay?"

"Yes. Do you want to speak to him?"

"Sure. I'll have the operator reverse the charges."

"Don't worry about it. Come, David. It's your Daddy in Honolulu. Here."

A loud crackle made John remove the receiver from his ear temporarily. His precocious 3-year-old son must have dropped it.

"Hi, Daddy," David said.

"Hi, David," John said, a lump of warmth in his

throat.

Only if he could hold him in his arms this minute, feel the soft skin, the curly little fingers, muss the fluffy hair, feast on the sparkling eyes.

"I went to Coney Island today with Grandpa," David said breathlessly, swallowing with the haste of narration. "We went on a carousel. I almost fell off."

"Were you on by yourself?"

"No. Grandpa sat next to me, but he forgot to fasten the seat belt."

"That was careless of him. But you didn't fall off?"

"They had to stop the machine, and the man came over and scolded Grandpa. Ha, ha. He is a dilly."

"So you are having fun?"

"Yes."

"Miss me?"

"I miss you, Daddy."

"I miss you, too," John said, eyes stinging.

"Is Mom with you?"

"No," John said. So that's what she must have told him. "But she'll be back soon. Be good. Listen to Grandpa, Grandma, and Uncle Sam."

"Okay."

"Promise?"

"Promise."

"Good. Now let me talk to Uncle Sam."

What had made her leave David behind and go to Korea by herself? To meet other men? Why not? He had practically driven her to it.

"Hi, John," Sam came back on the line.

"Did she say why she wanted to go to Korea?" John asked.

"To re-enroll at the Presbyterian Seminary on a full scholarship."

"Isn't that the place where Dr. Yonggoo Sohn is President?"

"Yes. He was her theology teacher there before she left Korea."

"I know. We hosted him and his wife when they stopped over on their way to Seoul."

"That explains it. One telephone call and everything was arranged."

"How was she, I mean, her health?"

"After the phone call she started eating again and was up and about in no time."

That was a relief. On the other hand, did it mean that he would not see her for three years or whatever it took to graduate from seminary? Maybe never? He doubted she would change her mind and return to him, even if he followed her by next plane and begged her on his knees. He couldn't blame her, either. In fact, it would be foolish of her to return to a jerk like him instead of making good her exodus already begun. After securing her by marriage with all kinds of promises, he had adroitly wiggled out of the chief one, her continued education for the ministry, by making her pregnant just in time as she received acceptance notices from both Harvard and Princeton seminaries. Using David as an excuse, he had wronged her and abused her, and was about to lose her. He was a rat and had it coming all along. But then everything came to a head with the fatal discovery of Angela Felini's letter in the drawer of his office desk.

How convenient it had seemed to have an office and a mailbox outside Hyangnan's surveillance! She searched his pockets and wallet at home, and clocked his every movement, but didn't think of extending the inspection to his territory on the University of Hawaii campus.   "Can't I have privacy?" he had remonstrated.

"What privacy?" she asked. "Husband and wife are one. The very idea of privacy, something unshared or unsharable, is contradictory."

She would even ask him what he was thinking.

"Nothing," he would say.

"You can't be sitting there, knitting your brow, narrowing your eyes, thinking nothing."

"Honest to God, I wasn't thinking anything."

"A spouse means someone to confide in totally. You must have been thinking about the countless other women in your life, including your former wives."

"Nothing could be farther from my thought."

"So you were thinking after all."

"Just about nothing - a cumulus cloud maybe, chirping insects, the surf, a crab crawling out of its hole between rocks. It could be anything."

"Tell me about those."

"You are really asking too much."

"You don't love me any more. That must be it. You are getting tired of me."

Tears followed, big, iridescent drops that melted his heart, forcing him to the ritual of recalling and inventing stories, metaphors and images, however fragmented or irrelevant. For the first few years he even enjoyed this radical scrutiny, which seemed to inject order and purpose into his amorphous life. Slowly, however, the restrictive regimen irked him, and he found himself spending more and more time at his office on various pretexts instead of rushing home to be near her.

"The Soviets have shot down the KAL jet, six hours after it left Anchorage, over the waters off Sakhalin," the State Department spokesman said on TV. "There are no reports of survivors."

Stunned, in a state of shock, John called the KAL Honolulu office.

"We are getting all the information from the networks just the same way you do, sir," said the manager testily, apparently repeating for the hundredth time. "After all they are trained men to do the reporting."

"Did I call you to lecture me? I am interested in the latest about survivors."

"There are none. Haven't you heard?"

"I don't believe it. My wife was on it."

"Oh, I am terribly sorry, sir. We'll keep in touch with you as soon as anything develops. Please give me your phone number and address. The Korean community here is also planning something and would like to have you included. The media will be interested, too."

"Publicity is the last thing I want," John said, hanging up.

But it came, the newspaper reporters and TV crewmen lining up at his door. He called New York. Sam answered choking with grief.

"Have you heard anything more than what the media is telling us?" John asked.

"No, but there must be some mistake," Sam said. "How can they shoot down an unarmed civilian plane?"

"They can and they did. The bloody Russians

have shot down with missiles. The plane just exploded and scattered into the freezing Siberian Pacific. How are your parents taking it?"

"They are both going out of their minds."

Honolulu had the nation's first anti-Soviet rally. Probably John's presence in their midst made them more sensitive.

"In the name of humanity and justice we denounce the barbarous murder by the Soviets of 269 people aboard KAL 7, one of whom...." an impassioned speaker broke down in tears, pointing at John.

"What have I done? What have I done to my Hyangnan?" John's mind kept swirling, as he stood dazed before the weeping crowd.

"Death to the murderer?" the ralliers cried, tearing, trampling, burning Soviet flags and Andropov in effigy.

The crowd dispersed and the Capitol mall on Beretania returned to its weekend desolation. Suddenly John felt the reality, the starkness of his loss. A wave of longing washed over him.

Just two months before their marriage he saw Hyangnan Char for the first time at her father's church, where John's mother was being ordained as Elder. Even so he wouldn't have gone there had his physician brother, ten years his junior but making ten times more money, not called from Los Angeles twice a day for a whole week, begging him to attend, saying "It means a great deal to Mother." He would have nothing to do with the congregation of janitors, dishwashers, bar girls, illiterate immigrants from the substrata of Korea, who were ruining the reputation of Korea, having come to the US as relatives of some whore married to a GI in Korea, who cheapened hard-earned US citizenship like his through student visa, graduate degree, professional employment, and five years of permanent residence. He had not gone to Pastor Char's installation a few weeks ago, though his mother had insisted, impressed by his credentials as former Chief of Chaplains for the Korean Armed Forces retired with the rank of Brigadier General. To John Pastor Char was just another illiterate Korean immigrant, who came to him for help with various church documents, his mother having volunteered her English professor son's services as usual.

Dressed in a green aloha muumuu Hyangnan sat before the organ, prim, austere, yet ineffably feminine, wholesome and refreshing like a morning breeze. One look at her sufficed. He had to marry her. Having arrived from Korea only a month ago, her family was sending her East to continue her interrupted seminary education. With her music and academic excellence they would snap her up. John had to forestall her departure from Honolulu at all costs.

Angela, a beginning graduate student with a former major in philosophy, was enrolled in his English class, and came to his office to comment on a class discussion or ask for his general philosophy on such varied subjects as World War III, shamanism, Oedipal complex. Treating every minor problem like a Ph. D. dissertation topic, she wrote those graders' nightmares, pages upon endless pages marshalling all the facts, documenting every argument with untiring impartiality, pedestrian persistence. Their sheer bulk defied easy faulting or dismissal. Appalled at having to write explanations for anything lower, John had to give her an A, which made her eligible for graduate teaching fellowship. Promptly, the chairman was sending him forms, asking for a detailed evaluation and recommendation.

He had enough on her to write a book. She had been living with George Harris, a black tennis pro. Before that she was married and had a Caesarian, which the baby did not survive, however. Her father was some wealthy investor in the East, and she had gone to the best prep schools money could buy. Then on a cruise to the South Pacific islands she met George and they stayed on in Hawaii. Her deep-socketed blue eyes burned like cold fire over the sharp aquiline of her Roman nose. Her tits pushed out from under the knit shirt stretched over her unbared breasts. Her leg dangled over the other knee. A tantalizing shag of fine gold hair carpeted her shanks and curving calves that flared into the parabolic mystery above the hemline, where his fantasy performed wild dances, while he discoursed on intellectually like a sexless guru with no taint of flesh or blood.

"Are you still with George?" John asked at their fifth or sixth meeting with the casualness of a demographer.

"Yes," Angela said.

"Everything's okay?"

"Yes."

"Loyalty and affection all the way, eh?"

"Yeah. He is good to me."

There was no breaching this rock of solidarity. But wasn't the very fact of her being in his office and her eagerness to have her lifestyle discussed and dissected the symptom of an underlying malaise? The confirming answer was not long in coming.

"The only thing that bugs me is that we can't go to too many public places," she said. "They gawk at us wherever we go, a white girl with a black man. I don't mind it but he can't stand it. So we stay home mostly. When we go out, we go separately like strangers."

"That's awful," he said, feigning commiseration, though inwardly glad at the opening crack in the armor.

"Hawaii is not the ideal melting pot that people think it is," he added indignantly, remembering how the numerically dominant Japanese in Hawaii threw their weight around, especially against Koreans. Many people in his church sold jewelry and gifts in Waikiki and had to pretend to be Japanese or at least something other than Korean: the Japanese customer would fold up his wallet and walk off upon discovery of the shop's Korean ownership.

"No place on earth is," Angela said with the weariness of an octogenarian. "I try to forget the world exists."

Then she began to drop notes in his mailbox. John replied, cautiously because tenure wouldn't protect him against charges of immorality involving his students. For all he knew she might be collecting evidence for blackmail or God knows what.

Next semester she was out of his class and was a teaching fellow, a colleague of sorts. He felt free to press his suit. But her defense seemed as impregnable as ever. One morning John was busy getting through a story for his fiction class at 12:30. Preoccupied with an overdue article, he had not looked at the textbook at all, postponing the necessary preparation till the last minute. Of course he knew the plot and a few general things about the story but to talk about it intelligently for an hour he had to review the material. There was a knock. Angela stood in the door with a woebegone face. Inside, there was the usual leg provocatively arched over the other knee, the forehead gleaming white like a crescent moon under the cascading gold. But visualizing himself as the unprepared, stumbling professor, all he could think of was the clock ticking away and the positive menace she was getting to be to his career.

"What's up?" he snapped.

"George and I quarreled," she said, apparently insensitive to his tone.

Or was he the consummate Oriental with an imperturbable exterior?

"What about?"

"I want to go away but he doesn't. He likes it here. Because it's free from prejudice, he says."

"That's a joke."

"I can see his point, though. The discrimination against his race on the mainland is something else, really. But I have to think about myself, too. I have to get away."

"Why?"

"It's stifling here. It was fun for a while, but let's face it. Hawaii is a resort to vacation in, not a place to settle down and do some serious work in."

"Depends on what you think is serious. For studying purposes one place in the Union is as good as any, postal and library facilities being what they are. Personally I would opt for a place like Hawaii - clean air, good beaches, temperate climate. Imagine being snowbound for months in Chicago or New York."

"But I don't want to study."

It was 30 minutes before class. There was definitely no question of his going through the assigned story and references, let alone eating his brown bag lunch.

"Are you aware of your physical charm?" he said recklessly. "Like a giant unconscious of his own strength, you stride on through the brush, not knowing how many twigs you break, how many bugs you tread underfoot."

"You mean I have devastated you with my charm?" she said, after staring at him incredulously.

"Yes. You don't know your own power," he said.

With a celerity of a pouncing lion he jumped up and embraced her. The class may go to hell! He could feel her wet body - under the armpits, between the legs soaking through his pants.

"I didn't want anything like this to happen," she whispered, pushing him back. "You are my intellectual filling station. I wanted it to remain that way. I can get this kind of thing anywhere."

"I sure don't get it anywhere."

"What's wrong with your wife?"

"A long story. All I can say is that if I had a choice, I'd never go through with it again."

Wouldn't he, though? Wasn't Hyangnan to be the end-all of his desire? With a shudder he recalled the department memo he had circulated inviting his colleagues to his "third and, positively, last wedding." Did he think he was being funny? On the contrary, it was nothing but puerile exhibitionism, obtuseness verging on retardation, coming from a 40-year-old professor. Why did he note his fiancée's age in parentheses after her name, "Hyangnan Char (20)"? So he must have thought it some distinction worth bragging about, his getting a bride half his age. A middle-aged man exulting in a young bride, like Chaucer's merchant! For days he took the seldom used stairwell instead of the elevator and chose odd hours to go to the mailroom to avoid his colleagues. It was enough to be getting their daily rejections through mail. How they must all resent him, John Minn, formerly Jongsoo Minn, the bungling Korean? Why inform them of his marriage, a means to solve a scatological need after all? He might as well have announced the hour and manner of his particular visits to the bathroom. He never learned, the eternal foreigner, never fitted into the all-white department atmosphere, always acted gauche, spoke with an accent. Whenever he saw two or three of them together outside the duplicating room, faculty lounge, before the elevator door, or in the hallway, whispering or laughing, he could swear they were discussing him, sniggering at the half man, the naturalized citizen mimic. Why did Hyangnan's folks put him through such ordeal? He had reasoned and argued with them, to talk them out of any big wedding.

"Far from being offended," John said, "your church members would feel relieved if you announced the accomplished fact the next Sunday after our wedding, instead of disrupting their routine or involving them in financial soul-searching, about the presents to bring. They'll truly bless us and respect you for making so light of your personal affairs."

"Make light!" Pastor Char exclaimed. "So you want to get off cheap on your third wedding and intend to have more maybe, because each time it's cheap and easy? In a ceremony of this significance, simplicity is not a virtue but an insult, a sacrilege. The tendency toward simplicity perhaps accounts for the secularity and debasement of matrimony and the consequent frequency and rapidity of divorce in this country."

Then Pastor Char came up with a clincher.

"Besides, you have to think of your bride's feelings. She has been to many weddings as piano or organ accompanist since she was ten, and has formed an idea of her own wedding, which I assure you is anything but simple. If she were in Korea, her wedding would be on a grand scale, attended by her friends and relatives."

John gave in. It was a once-in-a-lifetime affair for Hyangnan, and she might regret not having had a big wedding for the rest of her life. He recalled his long penance for not staying at the first-class tourist hotel in Pusan during the honeymoon with his first wife Sunhay, Karen and Allen's mother. He had genuinely detested the garish imitation of a Hilton on the Pusan beach and opted for the traditional inn up in the hills, cheaper perhaps but more tasteful and elegant, he insisted. But Sunhay never saw it that way. The cheapness was all she had noticed. As long as they lived together, she never lost an opportunity to remind him of it. No, he swore, not another Pusan honeymoon! He surprised, nay, alarmed his future in-laws by going all out in the opposite direction, renting the Hawaiian Hilton Ballroom, signing up the Royal Hawaiian Band, inviting his whole department.

A month went by before John saw or heard from Angela Felini.

"At least I would not arrive in class unprepared and hungry," he told himself stolidly.

Then her letter arrived: "It has taken a great deal of willpower to stay away from you but frankly you scared me off, though I appreciate your honesty. In the post-bellum angst, I couldn't handle the extra strain another commitment would entail. I've been off balance for some time. The dust is settling down gradually and I begin to see things in perspective. Helpful in this has been Carl Jung and his theory about Oriental meditation. I am attaching a copy of the paper I wrote for Dr. Gregory Pearson's criticism course, in which I point out...."

Poor Gregory to have to read all this dribble, John thought, throwing the 65-page opus into the trash can. But he decided to keep the letter as a symbol of his independence from Hyangnan, if nothing else. Titillated by the idea of secretiveness and betrayal, he slipped it in the drawer under the mass of papers - personnel action notices, bibliographies, recommendations, faculty memos, and forgot all about it.

Just before the finals Angela stopped over at his office and told him that she had broken up with George.

"I told him to move out, but he keeps calling back," she said.

"When did he move out?" John asked.

"A month ago."

"You've been by yourself all this time?" John asked, wondering at his negligence to exploit it.

"No, I met another man, a Vietnamese Ph. D. candidate in political science."

What was all that talk about extra strain and commitment?

"You go for them in all colors and sizes, don't you?"

"Yeah, he comes up to my eye."

"Has he taken George's place?"

"No, he doesn't live with me."

"Can I stop over?"

"No."

"Why?"

"Because I know what is going to happen."

"I might just surprise you."

"No, in this respect you are as predictable as anybody else."

"Can I call you?"

"Anytime. You know I enjoy talking to you."

In the whirlwind of activities at semester end, somewhat intensified by his forthcoming sabbatical, he dropped all thought about Angela. The prospect of not having to contend for a whole year with unmotivated students going through the motions for the diploma made him feel like starting his life all over again. Though he was not obliged to vacate his room completely for the next tenant, some visiting professor filling in for him, he was determined to leave nothing of himself behind. Anything less than total evacuation was not symbolic enough for his sense of termination and regeneration.

In her turn Hyangnan had been busy with the numerous spring recitals of the three choral groups, Honolulu Glee Club, Honolulu Symphony Opera Chorus, and Island Serenaders, to which she was accompanist, in addition to her usual stint as organist at the Korean church, her father's former church. Soon after their marriage Pastor Char left it and went to New York to head a big Korean church in Flushing, Queens. John had urged Hyangnan to quit the ethnic immigrant church, "the reactionary force that holds the immigrants back from integration into the American society and culture at large," as he put it. But Hyangnan was even more dedicated to its cause than when her father was around and wouldn't hear of moving to a regular Anglo church as accompanist at a bigger salary. For days John barely saw her at home and had been doing all the cooking, laundry, house cleaning, and chauffeuring for the children.

One evening, after supper, his family was together upstairs. Hyangnan at the piano for the next day's concert at the Waikiki Shell and the children engrossed with MASH on TV. This should complete the picture of domestic bliss and contentment for any man, but Satan would not leave him alone. John felt a sudden irresistible urge to call Angela. Tiptoeing downstairs, he dialed carefully, though it seemed unlikely, with all the noise, that anybody would hear clicks on the extension upstairs. On the third bell Angela answered.

"My God," she said. "I was thinking I'd never hear from you again."

"Could I meet you now?" John said, his pulse quickening.

Had the piano stopped? He couldn't tell for sure because of the ringing and thumping in his ears.

"I have meant to check my mailbox," she said. "The bus takes a while at this time but I'll be down in 30 or 40 minutes."

That was too long. He had to see her immediately. "I can pick you up at your apartment building," he suggested.

"You don't mind?"

"No."

As he was hanging up after getting the directions, there was a click on the line. He froze. Had somebody been listening or picked the receiver up and put it down finding it in use? Hyangnan? Heaven forbid! It couldn't be, because she would have run downstairs to ask who he had talked to, if she knew it to be a female. Sliding open the glass door downstairs, he went to the car. Hyangnan came darting to the upstairs window.

"Who were you talking to?" she said.

So it must have been Hyangnan who had picked up the phone.

"It was a friend."

"A friend?"

"She is from Los Angeles and I wanted to find out about conditions there."

He had been harping on the need to spend his sabbatical in Los Angeles near his brother and the Huntington Library rather than in New York where she wanted to be near her family, possibly also attending a seminary.

"She?"

Damn! It hadn't been her after all that had picked up the phone.

"Yeah, a former student."

"Where are you going?"

"To the office, to bring home some of the books."

"Take David with you."

"No, he has to go to sleep early and it'd bore him anyway."

John knew she was suspicious, but all he could think of was the impending rendezvous with Angela, who must be outside her building waiting for him by now. He had to get to her and no other consideration should interfere. Hyangnan was bounding down the stairs to intercept him. But with fierce efficiency he started the car, put it in gear, backed out, and roared off.

When he entered the office with Angela in tow, the phone was ringing. He hoped it was the first time.

"Are you alone?" Hyangnan asked.

"Of course!" John shouted, affecting offense at her suspicion. A quizzical expression on her face, Angela left his office to walk downstairs to the mailroom. Leaving the door open for her, John wheeled out a cartload of books to take to his car. Nervously he banged at the elevator button. At least a token load was necessary to explain to Hyangnan his precipitous departure from home, but every second away from Angela was criminal waste. Back at his office, Angela told him that her

Vietnamese friend Quang Tri Phu had left her or rather she had told him to leave. There was no time to waste over literature or philosophy, and certainly none for George Harris or Quang Tri Phu, though from the way she settled into the chair she seemed to be ready for a lengthy analysis.

"Let's get going. I'll drop you off."

"Don't you want to move more books?"

"No. They can wait."

At her building he asked her if he could come up.

"Only if you promise not to touch me," she said with acerbity that chilled him.

"On scouts' honor," he said. "But what's the point?"

"I don't want to get involved with a married man."

"Even when he doesn't mind?"

"I am a woman and I don't want to hurt another woman."

"But she need not know."

"I hate the sneaking around and lying. It's hell for everybody concerned."

"Let's go up."

"Promise?"

"Yes."

The protruding semi-elliptical balconies of the

units gave the cylindrical tower the impression of a corn cob. The 35th floor view included the ocean, Koko Head, Diamond Head, and Waikiki. She had told him she had a rich father, and the spread showed it - the plush carpet, splendid drapes and upholstery, tables and chairs of carved wood. There was an arrangement of fresh roses on the glass-topped coffee table before the sofa.

"From Quang Tri Phu," she said. "Sends me flowers when he can't have me. What's with men? When I am available, they treat me like dirt, can't be bothered because they are too busy writing theses, doing their world-shaking research, playing tennis, building their bodies. The moment I am offended and sulk, they are all attention and apology."

"The hunter instinct," John hazarded. "The male goes out to hunt and forage, brings home the catch for the female to cook and store away, then off he goes on another safari."

Was his observation to the point? Who cared?

"But women are as much breadwinners these days as men."

"The biological clock of evolution running way behind the technological."

Was he here to indulge her penchant for pseudo-intellectual discourse? Some other time maybe, but not now when Hyangnan must be calling the office. Maybe she might have asked a friend to give her a ride there to check him out.

"Angela," he said, looking at her. It was now or never. "It's getting to be increasingly difficult to keep the promise. Perhaps I should leave."

"Yes, you should," she said.

John went to the door and put on his shoes.

"Can I just kiss you goodnight?" he said, straightening himself.

"If you can promise it won't go beyond that," she said, with forbidding rigidity.

"I've kept my promise so far, haven't I?" he said, after some consideration.

"Yes."

"Try me again."

She nodded mechanically. Knowing the step to be the point of no return, he crossed over and pressed his lips on hers. Arms wrapped around each other, they fell on the sofa and got squeezed between it and the coffee table.

"Can't we go to a more comfortable place?" he said after some breathless exploration.

"Yes," she said, humidly, leading him to the bedroom.

Back at home past midnight, he was greeted by a storm of rage.

"Don't tell me you've been at the office all this time. I called every ten minutes. Where were you?"

"Downstairs. Talking to the guy who recognized me from the papers."

He had been written up in the local papers for his book, Life as a Refugee, based on the Korean War, which had been recently nominated for the National Book Award.

"What was his name?"

There was a total blank. Try as he might, he couldn't come up with a single male name.

"I don't remember," he said stupidly.

"The name is the first thing you ask of any stranger," she pointed out.

"This time I didn't get around to it," he said, feeling like a driver on a car skidding at 100 m.p.h., not knowing where he would crash land....

John managed to invent a goateed Hawaiian homosexual who had gone to New York, lost his boyfriend to another man, and returned home disillusioned and heartbroken.

"And he was waiting there all alone for you to show up?" she sneered.

"There was a meeting on Hawaiian culture," he said praying that she would not take it into her head to investigate. "At the Johnson Hall auditorium. During the intermission he saw me struggling with the books, came over, and helped me. We fell into talk."

Such a lame story! It didn't hang together at all, and he disqualified himself as a fiction writer. Hyangnan examined him for a trace of lipstick or perfume, and John was glad he had taken a shower at Angela's, using Ivory soap that presumably left no distinctive smell.

"Tell me the truth," she screamed, at the same time metamorphosing into a scratching, pinching, punching fury.

Immobilized by a sudden mood of resignation, John submitted to the punishment, neither ducking nor fending off. A particularly vicious twist and pull on his chest lit up a thousand candles and he was sure his poor little tit had been wrenched off. But even this was lost in the grand symphony of pain from the bruises and lacerations all over his body.

"What shall I do with you? What's going to happen to me?"

"Nothing. What's wrong with just talking to a homosexual?"

"Why didn't you call me to let me know?"

"I wanted to test you."

"Test what?"

"Whether you have full faith in me or not."

"You've never needed to test me. What testing is necessary between husband and wife?"

"I was in the mood for an experiment."

Mutual exhaustion brought them to sleep. Next morning they would have been at it again but were diverted by the timely visit of the Reverend Doctor Yonggoo Sohn, President of the Seminary. Normally he would have resented house guests, but this time the Sohns were a godsend. Gladly he met them at the airport, and showed them around - Round Top, Pali Lookout, Hanauma Bay, Blow Hole. The trouble between him and Hyangnan seemed to have evaporated in the ritual of playing host for three days as a cordial happily-married couple.

John and Hyangnan both went to his office for cleanup. She wouldn't send him alone any more. At 10:30 p.m. Johnson Hall was deserted and secured. John had to use the key to activate the elevator. Getting off the 4th floor, he told her to go to his office next floor up by herself.

"I'll be right up after checking the mail," he said.

"Okay," she agreed.

John heard the elevator door closing behind. Along with other mail, there was a note from Angela in his box, as he had surmised. The envelope had been half opened when he heard Hyangnan's footsteps outside. Hurriedly he jammed it into his pants pocket and let her in.

"The hallway was too dark," she said.

"Scared?"

She nodded.

"Nothing but junk mail," he said, handing her the bundle in answer to her inquiring glance and positioning himself sideways to hide the bulge in his pocket. He had to get away fast before she noticed it. She never missed the slightest wrinkle, the merest smudge or speck on his clothes.

"I must run to the restroom," he said, hugging his bladder and darting out of the mailroom into the hallway. She wouldn't dare follow him into the men's. But she might, knowing there was nobody in the building at this time of the night. He would have to shove the letter down the rubbish can and come back later to retrieve it. What if she tags along? He couldn't be going to the bathroom after such a short interval. He might have to take her home first, then sneak out after she fell asleep. That girl Angela with such an incredibly awful sense of timing! What could she possibly be writing about? The little affair that transpired at her apartment the other night? Why, they had fun, a moment of stolen pleasure, like picking a ripe mango off a roadside tree. That's that and should be the end of it.

"It was beautiful," he started reading the letter, a wary eye on the bathroom door. "I have no regrets. Having you after wanting you so much for so long was heaven...."

John tore it up and flushed it down the toilet. Hyangnan was patiently waiting outside. They went up to his office on the next floor by the stairs. She loaded up the cart and he took it to the car. After dumping the last load, he pushed the empty cart to the elevator and pressed the up button. His sweat-drenched knit shirt clung to the skin and his muscles ached. But he didn't mind. A wave of relief washed over him. With the office vacated, his duty to the department had been discharged and he need not return to campus for a whole year until next fall. During sabbatical he could go anywhere, finish his book without the interruption of class preparation and paper grading, fiddle on the roof, goof off. He got off at the fifth floor and walked down the hall to his office, humming, looking forward to a warm shower and a good night's rest at home.

The armchair squeaked with a violent swivel and Hyangnan flew at him, her face livid.

"What is this?" she shouted, shoving at him Angela's old note with that bit about Carl Jung's Oriental meditation. "Who is Angela? She is the Los Angeles friend you phoned the other night and spent three hours with, isn't she? You lied and swore up and down, until you ended up with a homosexual, as I remember. Did you think I would be so gullible as to fall for a fable like that? I've given up everything to marry you, to be a mother to your children. All day long I cook, wash, clean up, shop, take your children to school, flute and guitar lessons, pay bills, so you can be left alone to study without distraction, and you turn around and cheat...."

As the tornado of her wrath raged, John stood dazed. His mind went out of gear, out of whack, refusing to yield the simplest answers. Where was he? What was happening? How did she get hold of the note? How could he have been so stupid as to let such a thing lie around in the first place? Just in case, while Hyangnan was piling up the books on the cart, hadn't he positioned himself before the drawers, his back turned to her, for timely detection and disposal of objectionable material that might turn up? How could he have missed this damning evidence? From the partial tear of the note it must have been caught in the back of the drawer, escaping his notice. In spite of his reassurances the drawer was empty, she must have double checked with her usual thoroughness and looked deep inside.

"See it was written March 2," he said, pointing at the top of the sheet.

"So it's been going on for months, behind my back, while I was wearing myself out," she charged, fighting back angry tears.

"Look, Hyangnan," John said. "You are taking it all wrong. Read it over closely. It says I scared her off."

"You pushed her down to the floor, right here in the office," she said, her lips quivering.

"Nothing of the sort," he maintained. "You are reading too much into it. She was a student in my other class, a little pest bugging me for tutorial help. I was late for class that day. I had to get rid of her."

"Lying bastard!" she screamed, slapping his face. The blow seemed to clear his head. He went over the note. The only objectively culpable portion was the first few lines and they need not be given such incriminating construction, either. She was overreacting, totally out of proportion to the matter in hand. He could stick to this theory and ride out any judge or jury. But what good would it do? The world was not interested in his sordid deceptions and escapades. It was his home and marriage that was at stake. What mattered was not factual evidence but what she thought and felt. With unerring intuition she immediately made the connection between the note and the Angela he had slept with that night when he was supposedly discoursing on philosophy with the Hawaiian homosexual. She knew as surely as if she had seen the whole thing with her own eyes. An uncanny sixth sense led her straight to the truth, penetrating his deceit. Was it the full circle of nemesis catching up with him? After a few futile attempts to explain away the letter, John gave up and kept asking for forgiveness. She remained contemptuous, inexorable.

"All right," he said remorsefully. "I am no good. I am not worthy of you. Divorce me."

"I told you and I repeat it," she said. "I'll never divorce you. I'll never make David a fatherless child."

"You can remarry."

"And subject him to a stepfather?"

"Your new husband can adopt him and love him like his own," he said, though he knew by experience he couldn't perform what he preached to others so blithely.

John recalled his stormy second marriage to Tracy Fujimura, a third-generation Japanese born in Honolulu. He had bitter fights with her over money and other problems, but the primary obstacle was her two boys, at the time 11 and 9, who were to bear their father's surname, Fujimura, because he would never relinquish his right to them. They formed a sort of invidious aristocracy within their household, well set up with inheritances coming from both their maternal and paternal lines, whereas John's own, Karen and Allen, 5 and 4 respectively, were to remain the eternal proletariat. There was no way their lot would improve because his salary would always be considered an inadequate contribution to the luxurious life in that big house of Tracy's on Tantalus. After thirty years of such life Tracy's children would have everything but John's would have nothing to call their own. Had he been unreasonable in demanding equality for all the children? They kept accusing him of not loving her children enough because if they had been his, he would not have this sense of conflict or inequality. Perhaps he had been as biologically-bound as Hyangnan's folks who had objected to her marrying him with two children from a previous marriage. John could not stand two surnames in his household, and suffered from a constant sense of shame, inadequacy, castration. After much bickering, Tracy and John had to part.

"No man can love somebody else's child as much as his own," Hyangnan said.

"Do you still feel that way about Karen and Allen?" he almost asked but didn't. It touched them both too closely. They had fought over this very issue, his suspicion of her discriminatory love, especially after David's birth. Perhaps he should get a divorce after all. In Hawaii, either party can seek release without the other's consent.

"That's a damn Korean fixation," he said. "Haven't you heard of Americans adopting Korean War orphans, thousands and thousands of them, the abandoned flesh of Korea, treated like offal, like so many pounds of rotting meat? The mercenary Korean orphanages collected them like head hunters for the sake of numbers, to get US adoption commissions, CARE packages, and other post-War civil aid...."

While his lips babbled on, Hyangnan remaining unresponsive and unhearing, his mind strayed a few years back to the time when he tried desperately to overcome her father's opposition to their marriage.

"You got to be kidding, Professor," Pastor Char said. "You have children from your previous marriages. Hyangnan could be your daughter."

"Age has nothing to do with it," John said. "We are all physically compatible after puberty."

"That's the most monstrous, disgusting thing I've ever heard. Brutes, lower forms of life mate with their own young, but we are human beings."

"Hyangnan is not exactly my own young. I happen to disapprove of incest, too, for purely genetic, pragmatic reasons, though it is condoned in extreme circumstances by the Old Testament, a pragmatic document to be sure."

"Let's not add blasphemy to immorality. You think you are clever for finagling your way to the heart of an innocent young girl, don't you? But let me assure you it is no great accomplishment. Every dog that has topped a bitch has done as much. I thought an educated man like you would have aimed higher, providing encouragement and inspiration to bright young people like Hyangnan to become intellectual and artistic leaders in their fields, instead of cutting them down and appropriating them for your own selfish use as a stepmother to your children, as nanny and maid...."

"Would Jesus have turned away from stepchildren? Do you grudge a home to the millions of orphans from war, plague, accidents, broken homes?"

"The question is my daughter's marrying a man with two children, not a global issue. Natural motherhood is the universal norm. Even in your enlightened American society the courts award custody to mothers, not to fathers, as in your case. That alone shows your Korean bias, though you think you are more American than Americans."

Char had him there. Indeed in Korea the wife

joined the husband's family, her name entered into the family register and struck out when divorced, but not the names of her children who bore the father's name and belonged permanently in the family. When John divorced his first wife Sunhay, neither she nor John questioned the validity of this practice, although they had lived in the US over seven years. Besides, at the time John had such a low opinion of Sunhay as a mother that he had shrunk from the idea of Karen and Allen growing up under her tutelage, maybe well fed and fat but without any discipline or proper education. He thought himself infinitely superior as a parent and undertook the rearing of his young children, to regret it many times afterwards, to reproach himself constantly for not giving them enough of himself, playing with them, talking to them. He was too busy with his own studies, trying to write those absurd articles to look good to the department. When they came whimpering with a broken toy or a stubbed toe as the case may be, he invariably shouted at them for being careless, for not knowing any better than to bother him, the important, adult John Minn.

"My custody of the children is a given fact," John said. "There is no need to dwell on it."

"They need not have been motherless," Char

said. "You should never have divorced."

"That's like saying I should not have been born."

"They are two different things: in one there is choice, in the other there is none. Divorce is a crime against humanity. The great divorce rate in this country ...."

"One out of three."

"Only shows how morally, spiritually sick this nation is, which no amount of material advancement can make whole."

Why did he come to live here then?

"Even here divorce is still not the norm," Char went on. "I have seen successful marriages among Americans. Plenty of them remain faithful to each other, freely. To divorce, to undo such a basic decision of one's life as marriage shows a grievous lack of judgment, much worse than investing in bad business, buying the wrong house, going into the wrong trade. To divorce twice, as in your case, is proof that the person is incorrigible, incapable of learning from experience, of undertaking weighty actions with sufficient forethought. The first divorce may be blamed on youthful rashness or whatever, but to repeat it is simply unthinkable. Like being declared bankrupt twice."

"The second one was on a rebound, lasted less

than a year, and should not count," John said.

"What proof is there that your present decision to marry is not on a second rebound? As far as I can see, Hyangnan is bound for a life of misery, to be a divorced woman, bandied from one man to another."

"There's not going to be a third divorce," John asserted. "I have finally learned what love unto death means. The first marriage was arranged between the families. Sunhay's father was Speaker of the House in Korea, as you know. The second was similarly motivated. Tracy's father was a Federal Judge in Honolulu. The feeling I have for Hyangnan is different. I choose her and love her for her own sake, for her genius, her personality."

"How can you be so sure of your love in such a short time?" Char pressed. "The speed of it is frightening. What burns fast burns out fast!"

"Not necessarily, sir," John replied. "The sun came into being with a bang but continues to burn for billions of years."

"Inapplicable analogy!" Char snorted. "People need more than a couple of months to have any kind of marital conviction."

"Years could be compressed into a few days, even minutes," John said. "Extended acquaintance merely confirms first impressions. Compatibility is decided at first glance."

John then quoted famous romances, both historical and fictional, but Char was not impressed.

"If you love her so much," Char said, "why can't you wait for a few years until she finishes her education?"

Risk the chance of her meeting all those young punks at Harvard and Princeton?

"She can go to school married," John said. "Lots of students are married these days. Nurtured by a loving, supportive family, she would get her doctorate in record time."

"Not only would her education come to naught," Char predicted, "she would tire herself out into a jaded dray horse to be discarded."

*   *   *

Hyangnan started fasting. On the second day, she ran to the bathroom retching in the middle of the night. Yet, with astonishing willpower, she moved around doing her housework, then praying and reading the Bible.

"Is fasting a Char specialty?" John tried to taunt her out of it. "Remember your father fasting after the wedding was all set, invitations sent out, to make himself too weak to attend so Sam had to give the bride away? A lot did he accomplish, staying away from his own daughter's wedding, so he could say he had never sanctioned the marriage and squash the gossip that he was selling you out to a twice-divorced libertine and infidel. This way you are spiting, not serving, God. It's like chopping your hand off for an offering. God'd rather have you use it gaintfully and offer a tithe."

He badgered her some more but she didn't deign to answer. Then he begged her abjectly to desist, for the sake of the young ones.

"All it takes is simple admission," she said at last. "Tell the truth and all will be set right."

"Do you want me to say I have raped her?"

"The truth," she repeated.

"Even if I am guilty of the morbid things you imagine, shouldn't you forget the offense, forgive like a Christian you purport to be, and safeguard the integrity of this home, resume your role as wife and mother?"

"I haven't failed in any of my roles. Haven't I given my whole life to you, to your children, giving up my schooling, my youth, my prospects?"

At the next Sunday morning service, the fourth day of her fast, her piano accompaniment was even more inspiring. By skillful powdering and rouging, her thinness and paleness had been concealed. In fact, as she sat at the organ, she looked more radiant and angelic. John's heart ached to reach her and hold her. Why couldn't she just forget the little meaningless letter? Only if he could tell the whole thing, make a clean breast of it, as she demanded!

"Come off this insane course," John said.

"You know who put me there," she said.

Was this how Ghandi had bumbled the mighty British?

"What do you want of me?"

"Tell the truth."

"I have told you everything. There is nothing more to tell."

She turned away scornfully and stopped talking to him altogether. On Monday, the fifth day of her fast, her weight went down from 95 to 85 pounds. She was nothing but a wispy bundle. It wracked his soul to see her waste and wither. At night under the fluorescent light she looked positively skeletal. Her breath was weak and fitful, sometimes stopping for a whole minute. He almost woke her, to see if she was still alive, and to give her the confession. Then the faint breathing resumed.

"No," he steeled himself. "I shouldn't. Suspicion soon fades away, but hard evidence, like confession, remains history, to haunt and destroy."

When all his efforts to force feed her failed, he called his in-laws in New York. Both her parents flew over and took her and David to New York.

•   •   •

Like a hit and run driver caught after fleeing the scene, the first Soviet impulse was to lie about the whole thing. As late as September 3, fully three days after the incident, they said with a straight face, "We lost it; it went out of our air space." On September 4, confronted with more hard evidence, they had their Air Force General Romanoff admit to the Soviet planes intercepting something that resembled the US spy plane RC-135, though from the different size and shape even a retard would have had no difficulty telling them apart.

On September 5 President Reagan played the Japanese Defense Agency's tape recording of the SU-15 pilot's conversation with ground control, which established the pilot's clear perception of the airliner and his deliberate firing of the missiles, convicting Russia beyond a shadow of doubt as a callous, cold-blooded murderer. Yet, on September 6, the Soviet position was still denial and evasion.

When the Japanese tape was played at the UN Security Council with the whole world watching, the Tass admitted that the KAL flight had been stopped. On September 7, as worldwide indignation swelled into a crescendo of condemnation and revulsion, the International Federation of Airline Pilots refusing to fly to Russia, it admitted the destruction of the civilian plane, declaring that it had the right to defend its own air space. On the same day, at Madrid, Foreign Minister Gromyko blamed the US for hiring the 747 to do its dirty work of spying and causing the loss of lives. Another version of this scenario was given in Moscow that day by Chief of Staff Ogarkov, who, in medal-clustered uniform, claimed that the KAL plane had ignored 120 warning shots, though according to the corrected tape released on September 11 there was hardly time to fire a single warning shot.

This defiant self-justification became the official stance ever since. Telling all the applicants for compensation from the 17 nations involved to "go ask the US that's done it," the Soviets remained serene in their confidence that the whole thing would blow over and business as usual would return - a thought so repugnant to President Reagan that he devoted his entire weekly address to the nation on September 17 to its repudiation. But the unthinkable had happened. Immediately after the Presidential caveat, almost at a signal, the world's press dropped the matter, except for occasional references to the "black box," the plane's flight recorder, as if more evidence could do any good. Over a thousand effects had turned up, washed ashore or caught in fishing nets with their dumb appeal for vindication - a child's charred torso, a woman's body minus head and foot, a rib bone, thigh, abdomen, chunks of human flesh, ID cards with grease-soiled photographs. The unidentifiable female torso, covered with blond hair, was most probably that of Mary Jane Hendry from Canada whose ID was one of those recovered. At the month's end, the battery of the recorder gave out and all search efforts were suspended.

The Korean Airlines flew surviving families to Japan and ferried them by ship to the spot off the shore of Sakhalin where the plane had gone down. To throw wreaths into the turbulent foaming waters, to identify and claim the effects. John, his children and in-laws went through the display over and over, but could not find anything that could be connected to Hyangnan. As if she had seen to it that he, the recreant and reprobate, get no part of her in her death, that the severance between them be absolute and final. John stared into the haze of salt spray above the whitecaps shattering against the side of the ship. If only he could bring her back and tell her that he had really loved her, that he had been true to her in his own way because those infidelities had meant nothing! Wouldn't she, now disembodied, understand and wait for him to join her in the abode of all immortal spirits beyond the reach of evil or harm? Shouldn't he hasten and join her?

"Dad!" David shrilled, snapping him back to reality.

By reflex action John retightened his grip around his son's waist, balancing against the nearest stanchion of the careening ship.

"Let me down," David said, scrutinizing John. "I want to go to Grandpa."

"No, please, stay with me," John implored. "It won't happen again. I won't let go of you."

"Promise?"

"Promise."

"Okay, Dad."

Gratefully, blinking back his tears, John gazed into his son's face where he saw, miraculously, Hyangnan smiling back at him.

THE COURT INTERPRETER

I was at our Anaheim flower shop, cleaning up after my wife as she designed, when the phone rang. It was Bill Samuels, the attorney defending Mrs. Moonja Joo, the Korean grocer, accused of shooting to death a black teenager for stealing a bottle of orange juice. The case had become a cause celebre with the whole of black Los Angeles clamoring for their pound of flesh. As a certified court interpreter I had been mildly curious who had been appointed to interpret for the defendant, as she plainly needed this help, but had not given the matter much further thought. Los Angeles, insulated from Orange County by the sclerotic 5 or 405, held very little professional interest for me.

"How is it going?" I asked, recognizing his name from the papers.

"Not as well as it should. Not the least of my problems is finding a decent Korean interpreter. I have looked high and low in vain, when your name has been suggested to me."

"Can't you find somebody qualified in Los Angeles?"

"No, not the type we want, someone classy with the right diction and style to project my client as an educated, refined person, not some callous killer from a backward culture as the media has been portraying her. It's not just her who has this image problem. Every Korean immigrant is affected."

I knew without his telling me in so many words. It was so unfair. In total disregard of our shame and outrage over the seemingly senseless killing by one of our number, we were all being lumped together as a bunch of blood-thirsty mercenaries who didn't hesitate to kill our hosts just to make a buck. One Korean pastor I knew had even suggested that he and I collaborate on a letter to the Los Angeles Times, apologizing to the victim's family and friends, to the American society at large, explaining that as a people we were not given to such violence, that few of us knew how to use firearms, let alone carry them. We certainly didn't want the garden variety of muggers and robbers, be they black, white, or otherwise, to shoot us first, thinking we were all well armed and ready to fire.

Our corporate guilt, remorse, concern soon gave way to dismay and anger as the smear and hate campaign against Koreans escalated. Not content with closing down the Star Market by blocking its access and smashing its windows, the blacks marched the streets waving banners and placards that read, singular shifted to plural, "Go Home Killer Korean Grocers," "Deport Murderer Immigrants." Rap lyrics, recorded by popular black singers and sold in the millions, ridiculed and denigrated "Gooks, not born here, not speaking English, looking down on us, killing our kids." And the media lapped it all up, faithfully reporting their daily demonstrations, depicting us as pushy, crass materialists, holding human life cheap, obsessed with the goal to get rich quick, taking, never giving. The incumbent City Attorney, up for reelection and with political sights set on mayorship and beyond, ordered his deputies to get a life sentence, if not the gas chamber, for the reprobate. Other opportunists jumped on the band wagon, endorsing and encouraging the black hysteria. After all, the blacks had the head count, the votes. By now it had definitely become a matter of our national reputation, our survival, let alone our acceptance and advancement in the American mainstream, the dream of all of us with children born here, going to school, and making headway in their various professions and occupations. The victim was no longer Natasha Brook, but Moonja Joo and the entire Korean American community.

Coupled with this sense of threat was our revulsion and indignation as more facts about the Brooks filtered through the Korean language press, though unmentioned by its American counterpart. In fact, the grief of the family and friends, so telling on TV screen, appeared positively repulsive and obscene. The minister of the church the Brooks had been members of allegedly, who had displayed such genius in orchestrating the heart rending memorials and vigils for the young victim, hardly knew her. The loudly keening mother, the epitome of crushing maternal sorrow, had beaten and abused her daughter and turned her out of her house many years ago. Natasha herself, at the tender age of 15, was the mother of two children already, and had been living with her current boyfriend. Instead of pity for her or her orphaned children, she evoked with her enormous weight of 250 pounds orgiastic images of eating, mating, and breeding destined to unbalance global ecology.

We had to exonerate the accused, who had by now become a folk hero, especially among our small business owners, continually plagued by black shoplifters and other predators, for showing to the whole world that Koreans were no pushovers at their mercy. We had to fight back and reclaim our tarnished national honor. But how? We could only wring our hands in helpless fury, realizing that we didn't come across as eloquently and effectively as the blacks, that we didn't have their native English, their orators, artists, athletes, politicians, TV personalities, and other resources.

"We would like to have your services,

Professor," said Samuels.

He must have gotten my credentials from his Korean friends. Lately the Korean language papers had written me up, praising my fiction. I had resigned from the University of Hawaii where I had taught for 20 years. Both faculty and students had always looked on me askance, a non-native with an accent daring to teach English to the natives. Then there were the subtle barriers, the hesitations, doubletakes that made me self-conscious, ill at ease. In the two decades of my employment, I hadn't made a single friend in the Department. A few years before I quit, Yoonhee and the children were already in California, a move felt necessary to send the children to the schools in Lemon Heights, Orange County, where my physician brother lived. Public schools in Hawaii left much to be desired, and Punahou and Iolani, the prep schools that produced Ivy League material, were forever out of our reach. In the meantime the first flower shop Yoonhee had set up at Larwin Square near Lemon Heights was doing phenomenally well. It made more sense for me to stop commuting between California and Hawaii and become her full-time assistant. We sold and bought other businesses, went to live in Boston for a year to be with Brigette and Woodrow when they went to Harvard and MIT, and invested in commercial properties. Financial independence seemed just around the corner, when the recession struck, forcing foreclosures on us. With judgments hanging over our heads, we had to open our current flower shop, Orient Florist, in our daughter Brigette's name.

"Thank you for the confidence, but Los Angeles is just too far for me."

"We are prepared to more than double your normal fee to $1,000 a day."

The figure, though a fraction of what he must be charging for himself, made my heart skip a beat. I hadn't been making that kind of money since I left Hawaii, where indeed I could write my own ticket, up to $200 an hour for depositions. In a conference call with Korea I was paid $500 for translating one phrase. But in California the courts and lawyers treated interpreters like trash they could kick around at will, for $200 a day at most. For one thing, to service the huge ethnic populations with their aptitude for getting into trouble, an army of certified interpreters had to be maintained, on a pay scale palatable to the tax payer, which was minimal, lower than a laborer's. A profession, financially unrewarded, was no profession. In the popular conception bilingualism was a social problem, like poverty, endemic to the ethnic ghettos, to be overcome with tax money by harassed school districts and welfare agencies, not an art to be cultivated by lifetime study and dedication. Consequently the really qualified people, scholars, doctors, lawyers, and other professionals, stayed away from the demeaning role of interpreter or translator. I myself had also snubbed the state certification examinations of California for a long time. Apart from the lowly pay, the very thought of examination by some bureaucrats, novices and amateurs in the niceties of the vocation I had held sacred all the adult years of my life, was repugnant. What would they know about the agony of search for the exact equivalent in English of a Korean expression or vice versa and the ecstasy of discovery when the miracle was accomplished? It was every bit as artistic and creative as the poet's or musician's labor for the perfect line, perfect note. In time, however, I had to yield to Yoonhee's insistence on my getting the certification: it might come handy someday. It did, becoming the mainstay of our livelihood during the recession. With any luck, if the trial should last any length of time, I could earn enough to make our mortgage payments for some months without dipping into our ever-dwindling savings.

"But who pays?" I asked, knowing too well that the Joos must be bankrupt by now.

"The insurance company does, which also pays me," Bill said, guessing my thoughts. "Yes, she has been provident enough to maintain a sizable liability insurance for her business."

"But doesn't the court appoint the interpreter?"

"Not the ones the defendant pays for. Of course we need court approval, which is automatic in case of an active certified interpreter like yourself. The one we now have, certified and court appointed, is so bad that the court will be more than happy to see replaced."

"There is just one thing, the interpreter's fundamental duty of fidelity to the original. What is your client like?"

"She may not be the classiest lady, but then who is? Personally I don't believe one is intrinsically this or that, except as packaged and presented. She has had her hard knocks, even before this, but is quite a woman. She and her husband could get together a million dollars to qualify under the new US immigration policy for foreign investors. That's quite an accomplishment anywhere but especially in Korea. They could live comfortably there but decided to emigrate during the reign of terror under Doohwan Jun's Combined Investigative Board following President Junghee Park's assassination."

"You seem to know a lot about Korea."

"My wife is Korean."

So he had a personal stake in this beyond just the money he made as defense lawyer. His talk about the insult to the Korean pride, before mentioning my substantial fee, which would have been motivation enough for me, hadn't been just a line to bait me.

"I met Sunhee in Seoul where I was goofing off from college as a Peace Corps volunteer. Her father, a lawyer, was looking for an American tutor for her English before she went to the States to study voice. After threatening to deport me to stop our romance, her family finally consented to our marriage on condition that I go to law school and pass the bar."

"Fascinating! You should write a story about it."

"I haven't got the talent. Why don't you? We read your story GI Orphan. Interracial marriage is your favorite theme, isn't it? Sunhee will give you all the material you need in full detail. You have quite a fan in her. She was the one who went out and got a copy of your short stories after reading about you in the Korea Times."

"Thank her for me. Does she sing still?"

"No, I plead guilty to preempting her career and turning her into the world's champion wife and mother. We have three children, all musical like their mother."

"And will all pass the bar like their father," I

said, with genuine envy. I had been trying in vain to persuade my offspring to do the same, instead of just becoming educated bums with doctorates in public policy or history of art.

"Just out of curiosity how did you master English as you did? You write as well as our best writers, with no hint of foreignism...."

"But in speech I can't get over this accent. I was wretched about it for a long time but am resigned to it now."

"One has to really listen for it and, when discovered, it is pleasing, like patina to sterling."

"You are a great flatterer and we'll get along famously."

Bill had argued for the bail of his client, a propertied businesswoman who posed no danger of flight, but his adversary, Assistant DA John Moss, had his way. The magistrate set the bail prohibitively high, $2 million, to make sure that she stayed in jail for her trial. The mob wouldn't have forgiven them in case of her flight to Korea, a hinterland sanctuary for hardened criminals to the popular American mind, in spite of Korea's efficient police and extradition treaty with the US. But perhaps they did her a favor: the mob would have torn her to pieces, if only they could lay their hands on her through the protective jail walls. As a result, for her daily court appearances, she had to be transported in a police van under armed escort with other custodies, handcuffed and sometimes leg-ironed, in jumpsuits stamped LA County Jail on the back. From the loading dock at the basement level of the Superior Court building, they were herded to a barred elevator, remotely controlled, that took them to the holding areas on the different floors. From there the individual custodies would be taken via a maze of narrow passages to the smaller holding cages next to the courtrooms where they were to be produced. At this point, before entrance, the handcuffs or leg-irons would be removed, unless there was reason to fear physical outbreak. Also some considerate lawyers would provide their clients with a presentable change of clothes for a better impression on the jury. The custody defendants then emerged, one at a time through the side door, walking before the conspicuously armed bailiffs, who kept a wary eye on their every move.

My first meeting with Mrs. Joo was in the passageway by the holding cage for Department 72 before her pretrial hearing. We spoke through the inch-thick bars. She had just changed to a blue two-piece dress, her discarded jumpsuit folded in a pile on a shelf. The ordeal had taken a toll on her, dark rings around her eyes and a visible loss of weight.

Samuels presented the prosecution's offer: her guilty plea for life sentence with the possibility of early parole instead of the gas chamber.

"No, let's fight it," she said without a moment's hesitation. "I believe in the justice of this country. We wouldn't have come here without this faith."

"But it is human and errors are made," Samuels said. "Just suppose a mistake is made and we lose."

"We'll win," she said with finality. "I have full confidence in your ability."

Jury selection began. If guidelines existed about this business, such as the prosecution favoring the prosperous and conservative and the defense the poor and liberal, they flew out the window in deference to another overriding principle: racism. Both sides were intent on eliminating those who belonged to the race of the opposite party. Samuels ruthlessly weeded out blacks and Moss Asians or recent immigrants. However, to keep up the semblance of a search for an impartial and fair-minded panel, they routinely asked the prospective jurors whether they had heard or read about the case and formed an opinion, predisposing them to such a degree that they would vote in a certain way regardless of the evidence presented to them, which was followed by the predictable answer: emphatic denial.

Nobody would own up to being duped and manipulated by the media or being a racist. Amazingly in the first panel selected from the juror pool there were two Koreans, both first generation, one a mechanical engineer with McDonnel Douglas and the other a computer scientist with Hughes, both peremptorily avoided by Moss for inadequate comprehension of English, though in fact their English was quite good. The fourth or fifth replacement was a Japanese lady, Julia Tanaka, born and raised here, and wife of a police detective, with whom Moss found nothing wrong, obviously aware of the enmity between the two races, Japanese and Korean. It was Defendant Joo herself who told Bill to avoid her. The last survivors were 14 people, 2 of them alternates, 9 women and 5 men, all white, Anglo white, not even a Latino among them. So this was the secret of white success in the US. By default, because the minorities could not trust each other.

Trial began immediately that afternoon. In his opening statement Moss exulted in the overwhelming proof that convicted the defendant of murder. His first witnesses were the various law enforcement personnel. A firearms expert from LAPD verified that the bullet and the casing, recovered at the scene, matched the caliber of the pistol used in the shooting. The Deputy County Coroner, who had examined the victim's body, described, with the help of charts, the entry of the single fatal bullet in the victim's back a few inches below the collar bone to the left of the spinal column, between the fourth and fifth ribs, and its exit through the left ventricle and at the base of the left breast.

One of the prosecution's coups was the cassette tape extracted from the video camera installed at the ceiling over the counter to document shoplifts and holdups. Telling though it was, the evidence turned out a two-edged knife. Moss wanted to show just the portion where the defendant shoots the victim, "the relevant part, not to take up the court's valuable time," but Samuels wanted to be shown the whole three-hour reel, "not to take anything out of context." All or nothing it had to be. Judge Janice Wilson asked Moss if he still wanted the showing. Moss had to agree: if he refused, the jury would think he had something to hide in the rest of the tape. Lamenting its undue imposition on the court's calendar, already squeezed by this trial that promised to be long, the Judge ordered continuance to the next morning, since it was already past 3, the rest of the afternoon to be taken up in the disposition of other calendared matters, motions, sentencings and such like that went off in quick order.

The TV set and VCR were wheeled out on a cart and placed next to the witness stand. An audiovisual technician from the Sheriff's Department inserted the cassette into the VCR slot and pushed the play button. It was a typical afternoon at a neighborhood grocery store, uneventful and boring, with customers coming in and out, picking up their merchandise and paying at the counter. One juror sitting at the opposite end of the box from the judge's bench decided to create some diversion. He folded a sheet torn out of the pad provided by the court into an airplane and sent it flying to the middle of the courtroom, incurring a severe frown from the judge.

Then it happened. The lower right corner of the screen showed a hulking figure, tall and big, heading for the door with a gallon bottle of orange juice hooked in a finger, a loaf of bread, a bag of apples, and other packages under her arms and in her hands. Noticing, Moonja called to the exiting figure. The would-be shoplifter stopped in her tracks, hesitated, then strode over to the counter and confronted her accuser. Down came the gallon jug of orange juice over Moonja's head. A punch quickly followed, sending her to the floor behind the counter, invisible to the camera. Natasha turned to walk off like a gladiator who had just vanquished her opponent, when Moonja's head inched up from behind, followed by a flash of gunfire. Natasha tottered a few steps toward the front door, then fell to the floor. The whole sequence had taken exactly two minutes.

The prosecutor paraded a legion of eyewitnesses, 12, all black, swearing to have witnessed the defendant shoot pointblank in the back of the victim. If allowed, the whole town of South Central Los Angeles would have queued up to swear to the same, but the prosecutor wisely held the line at a dozen. Each time Samuels objected, on the ground that the defense had stipulated to the act of shooting and the trial should move on to the issue in dispute, namely, the defendant's psychology in so acting. The prosecution countered that they were about that very point, because the psychology of an action could not be determined except by examination of the manner in which it was performed. The judge overruled the objection and permitted the redundant litany to go on, though not without Bill's skillful puncturing of its effect. For example, one eyewitness claimed to have been at the counter when the victim fell at his feet.

"Were you in line already to pay for your purchases when the victim came over?" Bill asked.

"No, I was still shopping elsewhere in the

store."

"Exactly where?"

"It's been a while and I don't remember every square inch I trod. Do you?"

"Just answer the question."

"I suppose I was somewhere in the middle where the chips are."

"So you walked from there to the counter area?"

"Yes."

"Why?"

"There was some disturbance."

"Shouts and screams as the victim beat and mauled the defendant?"

"Objection!" Moss interjected. "Leading the witness."

"Sustained," the judge said.

"You don't have to answer the question," Moss told the witness.

"No, I don't mind answering. I didn't see any of that stuff."

"What stuff?"

"Beating and mauling you mentioned."

"Do you swear to that?"

"Yeah."

"Even though there is a videotape showing the attack?"

"Maybe the camera saw something I didn't," was the somewhat less strident answer.

"Would you be able to identify yourself among the onlookers if the tape were shown?"

"I can't tell until I see it."

Samuels did not press the issue further, however. The majority of the so-called eyewitnesses likewise swore only to the shooting part, not the battery and mayhem preceding it. One person was willing to admit seeing the antecedent attack by the victim, but when asked why he didn't think of intervening, he said he was "no bloody cop and minded his own business."

Bill called the defendant to the stand. My hour had come. Up to now, seated next to Moonja, I had been whispering a blow-by-blow report in Korean for her benefit alone. Now the whole world would hear her side of the story through my voice. This was the supreme moment, the culmination of my years of obsession with English ever since I was seven years old when Korea was liberated. English, the language of the Americans, the liberators, was the open sesame, and the interpreter, the high priest dispensing sacred rites. During the war years of the early 50's it literally meant the difference between eating and starving, between life and death. I still recall the time when Seoul was retaken by MacArthur's Marines after Communist occupation, three months of hunger and unspeakable horrors. A group of GI's sat by the roadside near our house eating C rations. Screwing up my courage I said, "I am hungry." One of them handed me a can of pork and beans. I ran with it to my house to share it with my starving family, younger brother and sister, mother, and dying father, a professor of English at Seoul University just home from Communist prison where he had been tortured beyond repair. Only if he could get up and tell the Americns in his fluent English that we needed food, clothing, and so many other things, and we would have everything, as in the good old days when Father got the big house we had lived in, the car, piano, and other luxuries. Despite our fervent prayers he died the next day. I had to master English, recover what he had lost. I had to make Moonja Joo credible, show her as the victim, not assailant, a law-abiding, hardworking individual outrageously and brutally attacked and abused, who had struck back as the last resort, to save herself. But how explain her shooting someone in the back?

Bill Samuels asked her name, address, date of birth, occupation, date of entry to the US, and motive for immigration.

"We had come to South Korea from the north and always felt like strangers anyway. We hated the division, war, fratricide, narrowness, dog eat dog of Korea and wanted our children to grow up in the big, open country that we thought the US was, where people of different colors and backgrounds from all parts of the world lived and worked together harmoniously. Then we read in the papers about a new US law allowing investment immigration for people with sufficient capital."

"How much money did you have?"

"A little over a million dollars from the sale of our house and other interests."

"What did you do with the money?"

"We bought the Star Market and a house here."

"How many employees do you have?"

"Ten including me and my husband."

"What are your hours?"

"Seven a.m. to 11 p.m. 7 days a week, but we arrive at 6 a.m. to get things ready and seldom leave before midnight, after putting away and cleaning up."

"On August 27, 1991, did you arrive there as usual at 6 a.m.?"

"Earlier, because we had to stop at the produce market on San Pedro Street. We had run out of lettuce and green onions the night before."

"What time did you notice Natasha Brook enter the store?"

"I didn't notice, because I was serving other customers and didn't look at the door."

"When did you first notice her?"

"I was reaching for cigarettes for a customer when I saw her walking out the door with a gallon bottle of orange juice in one hand and cheese and corn chips in the other. I didn't recall serving her and besides the merchandise was not bagged, so I called her."

"What exact words did you use to call her?"

"You mean in English?" she asked, turning to me, asking me, rather than the questioning counsel. It was impossible for the principals to zero out the existence of the translator, supposedly transparent.

"Yes, in English and in the exact tone you used," Samuels emphasized.

She looked around at the sea of American faces, cleared her throat, then said, in a somewhat hoarse unnatural voice, "Hey, you, come here!"

"Did you intend to insult her?"

"No, I had to attract her attention, let her know that I was aware of her trying to sneak out without paying."

"What did she do when you shouted to her like that?"

"She came over and stood before the counter, pushing everybody out of the way. Towering over me she yelled, 'Did you say something, Gook bitch?' I said 'No shoplifting.' All I heard next was a scream, because she struck me with the gallon bottle of orange juice in her uplifted hand. I felt the chill of the ice cold juice over my body and a taste of it in my mouth, when a punch to my face knocked me down. I struggled to my feet, half out of my senses, and saw her right in front of me. That's when I remembered the gun, the 38 Colt we had bought for $200. My husband had shown me once how to pull the trigger but I had no intention of ever using it. I picked it up and aimed at my assailant, just to keep her away so she wouldn't hit me again, but the next moment I heard the explosion. I didn't know about its hair trigger nor the removal of the safety pin by my husband while cleaning it the other day."

But all our effort to establish an unthinking, unconscious act on her part seemed to come undone by the prosecutor's cross-examination.

"After your arrest were you taken to the hospital for treatment?" Moss asked.

"No, I was taken directly to county jail."

"Did the arresting officers carry you to the car?"

"I walked on my own two feet."

"So the terrible beating you got from the deceased, which allegedly almost knocked your senses out, did not leave any open wounds that needed treatment, did not break any bones, did not cripple any of your bodily functions."

"No, but I had a lump on my head."

"Which nobody saw."

"My hair hid it."

"Do you wear any corrective lenses?"

"No, sir."

"You can see me without any problem, can't you?"

"Yes."

"Can you see me now?" Moss asked, walking toward the witness box. Directly before her he turned around and faced the courtroom audience.

"Yes," Moonja answered.

"Do you see my back or my face?" he asked, taking a step away from her.

"Your back."

"Isn't that what you saw on August 27, the back of Natasha Brook walking away from you, not facing you to resume her alleged murderous attack?"

"But I didn't...."

"Just answer my question!" Moss bullied.

After three days of deliberation the jury reached a verdict, guilty of manslaughter, which pleased neither party. Moonja was disappointed at the American judiciary that depended so crucially on a bunch of amateurish jurors, though Bill Samuels did his best to persuade her that this was a whole lot better than the conviction of murder the prosecution had been aiming for. On the other hand, already a murmur of discontent was heard among the blacks. Manslaughter which carried a maximum of 15 years in prison for taking a life, a young life at that? In smoldering anger they waited for the sentencing by the judge, who was given complete discretion by the jury. The sentencing was set for two weeks later but when the day came, Samuels asked for a month's postponement so he could research more and prepare appropriate responses, though it was the defendant's constitutional right to get speedy sentencing. This simple delaying tactic, he said, was to cool down the emotions involved, both in and outside the court, which generally worked in the defense's favor.

The sentence was three years, of which the defendant had served six months already by pretrial custody, the balance to be suspended. The reason: the defendant had acted under extreme pressure and was not likely to repeat the same offense, thus posing no danger to society. She was to be released immediately. She could go home, free. Her nightmare was over. If she had not been fully vindicated by the verdict, she certainly was in the penalty phase. It was a triumph for the defense, however one looked at it. If she had any reservations about the justice system of America, she had none now.

"We've done it, we've won," said Samuels, shaking my hand, eyes brimming.

He went on to be honored the trial lawyer of the year by the American Bar Association. I had my own payoff, too, with more calls from courts, lawyers, doctors, insurance companies, than I could handle. I could write my own ticket again. But our elation was short-lived. Nothing seemed settled, the DA's office having appealed the sentence. Besides one man's gain was another's loss. The verdict and light sentence was a slap in the face of black pride. Black demonstrators surrounded the court building and demanded the immediate dismissal of the white racist female judge. The police had to take her to and from undisclosed places, hotels and friends' homes, using unmarked cars, because her apartment was unsafe. Bill Samuels had to close down his office and even I had threatening letters in the mail and had to beef up security at home with two more dogs in spite of the great distance from Los Angeles. Black gang members plundered Korean businesses openly, robbed Koren shoppers and pedestrians in broad daylight.

But the worst was yet to come during the Los Angeles Riots that erupted soon afterwards, on April 29, 1991, upon acquittal of the four white

LAPD officers accused of beating Rodney King. The white policemen who had seemingly used excessive force in arresting King were all let go free by a predominantly white jury in Simi Valley. This was just one verdict too many, demeaning black life and dignity. Angry crowds gathered at the LAPD headquarters. Held back by the phalanxes of policemen, they vented their rage by overturning the information booth in the parking lot and smashing and stamping on it. Then the gas station at the corner on the same block as the LAPD building was set on fire. Next the news camera showed a building on Normandie in flames, the very building where Moonja's Star Market was located. Another fire followed on the same street. Soon fires were everywhere and engulfed the whole of Koreatown. To save themselves many building and business owners were hanging out signs, "Not Korean owned." Looting began. Mobs broke into businesses, stores, offices, and carted off everything they could lay their hands on.

We were mesmerized by the live TV coverage of anarchy and violence that swept through Los Angeles like wild fire. Whole blocks were going up in flames but no fire engine came to put out the conflagration. No police were around to stop the beatings, lootings, killings so vividly reported on

TV. Suddenly we remembered Yoonhee's brother Chanho, his wife June, and five-month-old son Charles living in an apartment building in Koreatown near 9th and Vermont. We hadn't communicated with them for months since they left Orange County. Our parting hadn't been pleasant exactly. In fact, quite the opposite. The Korean restaurant he ran at our commercial property near Disneyland failed and he blamed us for his losses, demanding $20,000 in compensation. His point was that he wouldn't have left Hawaii, if we hadn't painted such a rosy picture of business prospects in California. He wanted us to pay for his moving, wife's maternity, and loss of wages and profit. When we refused, he kicked over furniture, broke glasses and dishes, even threatened to shoot us.

Yoonhee dialed their home number repeatedly but nobody answered. Several frantic calls to Hawaii gave us the number of Hanyung Jo, one of his friends from Hawaii, who lived in Glendale 15 miles from Koreatown. Hanyung said Chanho was bringing his family to his house but was probably being delayed by the roadblocks. We kept calling every other minute. Finally, at midnight June answered. Chanho was not with them. After dropping them off at Hanyung's he went back to town with a gun to guard the stereo shop where he worked.

"A gun!" Yoonhee shrieked, vaguely recalling his threat to shoot us. So he must have meant it. How close that had been! "When did he get it?"

"As soon as we came to California. He's been going to the gun club and is a pretty good shot."

"Why didn't you stop him? He's sure to get hurt." "He says he owes it to the owner who treats him like his own son," June answered unruffled. Was it a veiled reproach to us? "You know he has a lot of loyalty."

"Loyalty to what? He should be with you and protect you, not a measly job."

"Well, I can't stop him when he makes up his mind."

"If you don't, I will," Yoonhee declared, hanging up.

She wanted to drive out to Koreatown instantly and tear him away bodily from the stereo shop, but had to abandon the plan. The news showed cars stuck for hours in the freeways accessing Los Angeles. We tried to call June again but the line was busy all night. We fell asleep, exhausted.

The phone jangled us out of bed the next morning. Choking with tears June said Chanho was in intensive care at Cedar Sinai Hospital with a gunshot wound to his head. He didn't regain consciousness and died a week later. After burying him and dropping June and Charles at their apartment, we drove down Olympic flanked by gaping reminders of the Riots. We had paid for his funeral expenses, only a little shy of the $20,000 he had claimed we owed him. Only if we had given him the money, so he didn't have to go to live and work in Koreatown!

As we turned south on Normandie a sickening vista of destruction came into view. Nothing remained of the many Korean-owned businesses on the block, liquor store, beauty parlor, laundry, flower shop, bakery, restaurant, indoor swap meet, and Star Market, in particular, a pile of charred rubble. Did I do her a favor, rendering her worthy of sympathy and respect? Shouldn't she have gone to prison, even to the gas chamber, condemned and undefended, for everybody's good, even her own?

Suddenly it became as clear as day: I had caused it all with my English as a second language, a little game I had played for a mercenary motive, to please my vanity. I was the arson and looter responsible for the billions of dollars in property damages, the mass murderer of Chanho and 52 others, who would still be alive, had it not been for my contemptible bilingual manipulation.

"What's the matter, honey?" Yoonhee asked, as I pulled over to the side.

"Nothing, just a headache."

"You sound terrible. I'll take the wheel. Maybe you have an attack of allergy from all that standing around at the cemetery."

"Maybe," I mumbled, unbuckling.

MOONBAY

Daro Jo kept walking along the waterfront of Honolulu. The Yacht Harbor, boasting the world's best maintained slips, with four or five year waiting lists, slumbered with the sweet, self-induced exhaustion of those who could afford the sea as a plaything. Night lights blinked, keeping drowsy watch along the piers, while their white-painted tenants tugged at the moorings as gentle ripples caressed their sides. A hardly perceptible stir of wind stroked the calm sea and a half moon played hide and seek with the lazy sway of coconut fronds silhouetted against the dark background of the Koolau Range to the north.

The Aloha Tower, formerly the hub of worldwide sea traffic, hosting luxury liners, was a museum piece, targeted for school excursions. Piers 17 and 18 had a retinue of tumbledown, dilapidated fishing vessels with their baskets and buoys, mostly Korean-owned and operated, because no other ethnic group would endure the physical rigor of longline tuna fishing with such woefully inadequate equipment. Their accident proneness was well known to the US Coast Guard which expected every other distress signal to be from a Korean boat. Nevertheless ready cash attracted the Korean immigrants who could not get any other jobs, especially during the recession which seemed to have hit the tourism-dependent

Hawaii hardest. Daro had resolutely kept away from those barely seaworthy tubs, substandard and illegal even in Korea but strangely tolerated in the technologically advanced US because the fishing lobby in Washington opposed all government intervention.

Beyond the Shell and Standard oil refineries, Daro reached the Foreign Trade Zone where vessels of foreign registry docked. Hours on foot, he barely noticed where he was. He had failed at land jobs, which sailors yearn for every time they cast off leaving the security of land. Perhaps everybody had his God-given calling, deviation from which spelled disaster. Daro had sworn never to return to a sailor's life, but here he was, at least his subconscious was, looking for a maritime job. But the merchant marine was plagued with chronic unemployment. There was no ferry, not only between Hawaii and the US West Coast, but even between the islands. The few attempts to put an inter-island ferry into operation, such as the state-subsidized hydrofoil Seaflite, had failed miserably after a few months of trial. It was the age of the airplane, and even the heaviest dead weight was air flown. Few considered the sea a viable means of transportation, either of humans or of cargo. Why hadn't he been trained to be an airline pilot instead of a sea captain and navigator? Daro felt prostrated by a sense of misplacement and anachronism. Wasn't he an antediluvian freak, surviving the Flood and unnecessarily burdening the earth? A sudden weariness came over him and made him long for release, for surcease.

He had certainly paid his initiation dues as immigrant in Hawaii, five years of it, working at the most menial jobs - laborer for construction firms, dishwasher, custodian, gardener - none of which lasted. Most recently he was a maintenance man at Schofield Barracks with the 25th Army Division but the Korean custodians there resented him for not joining in their picnics and get-togethers.

"The stuck-up son-of-a-bitch thinks he is a haole or something," they whispered among themselves referring to his slightly Caucasian features. With a complex about their language and lifestyle, their nationality, culture and heritage in general, these expatriate Koreans, condescending, contemptuous, or spiteful to each other, were nevertheless compulsively gregarious, and were unforgiving to a loner like Daro. It wasn't long before he found himself out of work.

But Daro didn't hold it against them. How could they understand his need to be left alone, his fear of being hurt again by getting close to people, any people? Immigration to the US and life as a foreigner had seemed the nearest thing to the isolation he sought, contacts with foreigners in the distancing medium of English posing no threat. He had chosen Hawaii, thinking its insularity an added protection. But Hawaii was desirable to other Korean immigrants, too, who seemed everywhere, especially in the lower echelons of the Honolulu social hierarchy. And they would not leave him alone until, with the insidious tool, Korean, they pried open and laid bare his soul to its raw wounds.

He rounded the huge warehouse in the center of the Zone, bounded by Piers 39 through 41, each three or four city blocks long. An Australian freighter was unloading. Cranes emptied big buckets of sand over a mountainous pile on the dock and huge loaders with tires the size of pickup trucks worked furiously to fill up and send on their way the waiting 50-ton tandems.

It was long past midnight, but on the deck of a ship tied at the end of Pier 41 men were up and about, shouting, though the roar of the equipment pushing the sand drowned their voices. As he came closer to the 1,000-ton longliner, Daro knew at once that the crew were Korean in spite of the un-Korean name San Pedro painted on the bow. His astonishment increased when the moving figures seemed familiar.

The man pacing on the pier at the foot of the gangplank as some sort of sentry stood petrified at the sight of Daro. Slowly recovering, he looked up at the deck, then back at Daro. Gingerly he started walking toward Daro for a closer inspection. With recognition his jaw dropped.

"You gave me quite a turn, sir," he mumbled. "I thought you were .... Imagine seeing you here, Captain. I am Sungchol Byon. You saved my life, remember, sir? I heard you had gone to America but didn't expect to run into you here of all places."

Daro had rushed Byon to a doctor in the middle of a successful squid operation in the Tasman Sea. It was perhaps foolish to suspend the work, especially when the whole sea boiled with squid. The slimy creatures, attracted to the floodlights along the sides of the boat, clawed at the rotating lines and dropped on the deck like popping popcorn as the mechanized pulleys kept turning the lines like a conveyor belt between sea and deck. A few more nights like that would give them a full load and they could be heading home. Then Byon, 21, passed out at his post by one of the pulleys, delirious with a fever. When the boat had touched at Tarawa for refueling, he and his companions had gone to a native village to have pearls sewn into their foreskin. Apparently the operation had been successful with the others, but in his case the pearls caused a horrible infection which spread to his kidney and lower abdomen. But even in this predicament he had been too scared to report and his accomplices were equally silent about it, according to their pact. The whole thing was to increase their sexual potency and desirability, especially to the white whores when they should stop at an Australian port as promised. The pearly knobs would more than make up for their small size. Of course their success at home with their own women would be phenomenal.

"How come you are here yourself?" Daro asked.

"With the ship, sir," Sungchol said, jerking his shoulder to indicate the San Pedro.

"Korean ship?" Daro asked.

"The Daywang Fisheries runs it, sir."

"When did you arrive?"

"Yesterday, sir, for refueling and supplies and ...." Sungchol checked himself before resuming gratuitously, garrulously. "Actually, Daywang got the ship on loan from the Mitsubishi Marines of Japan, which got it from Nicaragua, which got it from Spain, which got it from Russia where it was first built. We were on our way to rendezvous with the mother fleet near Mexico. We unloaded a full load of skipjacks at the Sunkist packing plant on Samoa. The ship's as big as the flagship Daywang and can be on its own away from the fleet."

"Who is the captain?"

"Moonbay, sir."

Daro was stunned, as if hit by a hammer, and remained speechless, unable to get over the shock. What perverse fate had led him to a ship commanded by Moonbay? The intervening years had not diminished Daro's abhorrence of the man, evil personified, contaminating and spoiling everything that came into contact. Slowly, like a marionette rewinding, Daro turned on his heel and started to walk off.

"Captain," Sungchol grabbed Daro's hand. "Please stay and do something for the trouble we have aboard. You know how rotten Moonbay is. He has cheated the crew out of $30,000, their share of shark fin sales."

To any longline operation the sharks were a nuisance that had to be cut off the lines, more sharks getting on the hooks than the tuna, but when the hold was full and the crew had time on their hands, the sharks were hauled in for their fins, which were cut and left hanging to dry on lines above deck. Sometimes the whole topside would be covered by lines and lines of drying shark fins that resembled the cooling system of a giant radiator. In good weather it took three or four days to dry to paper crispness, the quality the dealers wanted. A dozen sharks made five kilos of dried fins. Shark fins or other catches in excess of the full hold belonged to the entire crew, including the captain, and were distributed among them according to rank, the captain generally taking five men's share, while the first officer and engineer took four, and so forth. Though shark fins were contraband in the US, Moonbay had connections in Honolulu and sold all the three tons of shark fins, $8 per kilo. Of course absolute secrecy was required and only Moonbay handled the entire transaction. Though they had their doubts, the man had to be content with their share of the alleged proceeds, $24,000. Moreover, it was Moonbay's practice never to grant shore leave to the crew, officers included, though he himself didn't remain aboard whenever the ship was in port. However unjust or irrational, he never retracted an order once issued and enforced it with fanatic rigor, beating the men for the smallest infractions. Since open defiance would be punished as mutiny, the crew had to devise circumventions whenever they could get away with them. The result was a vicious circle of mutual abuses and deceptions which somehow restored the equilibrium.

Moonbay left the ship the night before, saying as usual that he would be only a minute and would check back momentarily to make sure that nobody had left the ship. Indeed he always phoned back in the middle of the night to see whether everybody was aboard, but this would be countered by choosing somebody to stay behind to answer the radio call. Moonbay took the receptionist's word for it and did not go as far as to wake up everybody for roll call. However, the crew was prepared for this emergency, too. They had a cassette tape made recording every crewman's voice, identifying himself "Aye, aye, sir, Seaman Shinjo Tak reporting. The moon hangs askew, sir," or some such sleepy nonsense to lend credibility. So even in the worst case all the man on duty had to do was find the spot where the man's voice was located, and play it to the transmitter. The time it took could easily be explained by the lateness of the hour and the proverbial deepness of a sailor's sleep. On no occasion had it been necessary to resort to the tape expedient, however.

That night, with the extra cash from the shark fin sale burning in their pockets, the men were all anxious to go into town, especially to the famed bars of Honolulu. First Mate Noga Kim offered to stay behind and told everybody else to go on shore. Sungchol, pleading a headache, also volunteered to remain aboard, for a purpose. With Noga's knowledge Sungchol had managed to stow away four kilos of shark fins under the ship's water tank. As soon as the others cleared the ship, the two conspirators took the bundle in search of a likely place to dispose of it. While filing papers with the ship agent at Samoa, Noga had learned that a waterfront bar called Bora Bora entertained smugglers from the foreign ships. They looked for it on Nuuanu Avenue. After discreet inquiuries the proprietor of the bar got on the phone. An hour later a Chinese dealer, a thin diminutive man with a sparse goatee, came to the bar.

"Are you from the San Pedro?" Ah Sing, the Chinese, asked after the introductions.

"What if we are?" Noga said.

"Because I just bought three tons yesterday from your captain and he swore that was all he had."

"Well, he forgot about another couple of tons, of which this is the sample. How much can you give us?"

"The same price."

"What is that?"

Ah Sing flashed a suspicious glance at them.

"I mean these are much better samples, better

dried, thinner, tenderer," Noga added hastily.

"Looks the same to me. In fact, because I have bought three tons already, I don't need any more. The new batch will have to be $2 less per kilo."

"Take this lot at the full price and we'll bring back the remainder if the discount is agreeable to the rest of the crew."

"It's not the captain who decides?"

"We are all in it together."

Ah Sing paid out $72, $18 per kilo, ten dollars more than reported by Moonbay. Noga and Sungchol picked up most of the San Pedro crew from their various haunts, and briefed them on Moonbay's treachery, taking care to omit mention of their concealment of four kilos that led to the discovery. Nobody cared about the process. Only the result mattered. The crew returned to the ship shouting murder. Nevertheless, though they had hated Moonbay, the whole affair could have been settled with apologies and restitution, but it was Moonbay's style to ride high and mighty over his men, no matter how much he was in the wrong. The phone rang about 3 a.m. Moonbay was furious because nobody had answered him when he first called about midnight. As might be expected, Noga answered his skipper less than reverently and Moonbay was screaming on the radio, swearing he would teach him a lesson when he got back to the ship.

Moonbay returned, raging, but was somewhat dashed to see the crew lined up on deck, not at all impressed by his wrath.

"Is it some kind of mutiny?" he bellowed. "I will teach you bastards manners."

He swung his fist to hit the first man, Inho Kim, a former veteran of the Special Unit, Korean Marine Corps, Vietnam, a blackbelt in tae kwon do and quick in his reflex. Dodging the blow Inho seized Moonbay's outstretched arm at the wrist and elbow and, using the momentum, pivoted the assailant on the arm socket, throwing him flat on the floor. All the crew rushed on the fallen man and started kicking and mauling, until he sprawled, bloody and unconscious.

If Daro had not arrived in time, perhaps they would have finished him off right then and there. With difficulty they were persuaded to hold a court of inquiry first. A bucket of sea water emptied over him revived Moonbay, who freely admitted his guilt when confronted with the evidence.

"I was exercising every captain's prerogative," he said, unrepentant, undaunted.

"You aren't a captain, you louse," the court said.

The verdict was guilty and the sentence was dunking, something slightly worse than keelhauling, which some of the crew wanted to execute instantly. But caution prevailed, especially with the ship agent radioing in all clear from the customs and harbor-master's offices for departure. Why risk the chance of the body surfacing in Honolulu Harbor, when they would be in open sea shortly? There was, however, one disturbing factor: a gale force wind had started blowing from the northeast, threatening to get worse. The sea lanes were crowded with inbound ships seeking refuge. Did they really want to leave port? the ship agent asked. Yes, Noga and the crew answered. Moonbay booted down the hatch into the hold, the crew bent to the total effort of getting the ship under way out of harbor.

"The harbor pilot won't be there for another hour," the ship agent said.

The cluster of officers in the cabin looked to Daro expectantly, then made way for him to take the helm. Nobody seemed to remember such trivia as his going home and picking up his papers, change of clothes, and other personal belongings.

"We'll manage on our own," Noga said.

"Good luck and bon voyage," the agent signed off.

The engine purred, as if in glee at the reactivation. A superbly maintained ship, she handled well, responding sensitively.

"The son of a bitch takes care of his engine," Daro admitted, grudgingly.

The thrill at the sense of power was like a heady drink. He was at the top of the world. Everything made sense now. Gone was his depression, hopelessness. A new purpose guided him. He was a born sailor, back in his element, and nothing was to deflect him from his vocation. His heart overflowed with thanksgiving at his reinstatement and the towering waves that battered the ship, twisting and flouncing her in wanton fury, only exhilarated him. The crew, veterans of many years' seamanship, were in mortal fright and despair at the ferocity of the ocean, which showed no sign of abatement day after day. But at no point was Daro uncertain. The years of disuse had only sharpened the edge of his expertise. The storm was a mere reorientation course with its prescribed obstacles and maneuvers. He had been through them before, much worse ones in fact. His confidence in the safe outcome of the voyage was never shaken.

One morning, the sea still churning with whitecaps though the storm was officially over, Moonbay was brought to the deck where the entire crew had assembled. The prolonged confinement in close quarters had told on his unusually robust constitution. His face, overgrown with stubbles of beard, was dull lead, his eyes blood-shot, his wrists and ankles swollen from the ropes that bound him, and his whole body covered with ominous bruises. To see him so degraded was strangely disconcerting, though everyone of the crew had cause to exult in his downfall. Perhaps it was vanity, for there was no glory in triumphing over a wreck like that. Or perhaps it was the sudden flash of insight into human frailty and mortality, into their own vulnerability. Did anybody have the right to punish and torment a fellow human being, no matter how great his offense? Who would cast the first stone? For a long time the men stood undecided, as if mesmerized by the awful sight of the broken man, once proud, vain, crafty, cruel.

His animal cunning must have perceived the subduing effect the sight of him had produced on the men. He affected a more pathetic, dead appearance, though through the slit of his eye he busily looked for an opening. Then his eyes rested on Daro. Finding him there after many years didn't seem to surprise him. The only thing that concerned him was whether Daro was the weak spot he needed to break out. He decided it was. Quickly erasing a smile that curled his lips, he lifted his hand wearily and pointed at Daro.

"Let me talk to him," he whispered.

Those near him jumped to their feet and passed the word. As soon as Daro came over, Moonbay motioned the rest away.

"You see how they cower, the scum," Moonbay said contemptuously. "I'll throw them all to the sharks. Mighty glad to see you in my hour of need. You are on my side, aren't you? You won't let me down. We have meant a lot to each other. We even look alike."

Daro listened, amazed at the man's total freedom from conscience or memory. To Daro's chagrin the physical resemblance, a pure coincidence, had been there, compelling him to deny their consanguinity whenever people remarked on it as they grew up together in the same village. In contrast, Moonbay had always gloried in it, telling everybody they had been brothers with supernatural paternity, somewhat as in the immaculate conception of Christ. Both their fathers were cuckolds, though they didn't know it, Moonbay said. Daro had hated him for making up such fiction and wanted in vain to get away from him. But some strange fate seemed to throw them together all the time. They had gone to the same schools, including the Maritime and Fisheries College in Yosoo, and even got the navigator's licenses at the same time. What did he propose to accomplish by referring to this quirk of nature at this particular juncture with the whole ship watching them? Could he have forgotten what he had done to him? Could a human being deliberately stab and poison another human being and erase the memory of it clean from his mind? Could his devious, amoral mind be thinking that his seduction of Nan, Daro's wife, had bound them in some kind of kinship, "holing partners," as the crude Korean saying went to describe men who had shared the same woman? Oh, Nan, how could you have fallen for such a wretch!

Daro recalled with pain his return from a 15-month voyage to the Atlantic, near the Spanish coast. It had been a lucrative trip and he had bought a lot of presents for Nan from Lisbon, the cheapest shopping capital of the world, a Gucci handbag and a whole lot of name-brand toiletries, accessories, perfumes. The trip home was made a little precarious as they encountered cyclones in the Indian Ocean and Daro had considered quitting sea life for good to find some steady land job, so he could be with Nan all the time. Arriving at his apartment by taxi, he let himself in noiselessly with the key he still carried around on him. She was bent over the range cooking something. Her mother, who lived with them, was preoccupied with her ironing. His heart nearly burst with the wild flood of his blood. Silently he went up and clasped Nan from behind.

"Moonbay?" she had said.

His blood froze instantly. His hands fell down his sides like dead weight. She turned around and let out a scream when she saw Daro. Then, as he stood gaping at her inflated abdomen, she dashed past him and ran out of the apartment to jump off Daysoong Bridge, the impact killing her instantly.

"Let bygones be bygones," Moonbay said. "We've been through a lot together ever since we were kids. I have always valued you as my own brother, my own self. More than once I've risked my life to save you. Remember the time when you fell and got stuck on the ledge of a cliff at Mt. Sorak and nobody else dared to climb down with a rope?"

"Does that entitle you to my wife?"

"Listen. Why torture yourself over a mere woman? We are men and what we mean to each other man to man counts. Women are a lower species than us. They are everywhere for the taking. It's silly to be attached to any one of them. I can get you any number of them, of any color or race. Just get me out of this jam. You can do it if you want. They look up to you. I won't forget it. In fact I'll repay you with my life."

"Do that," Daro said, turning away in disgust.

His rejection of Moonbay nerved the assembly

to their unfinished job. There was no trifling with a man like Moonbay. Their charity, if indeed they were capable of it, would be returned with dire retribution. Besides pity was a fragile motive. Money and revenge were the more powerful and stable influences that asserted themselves in the end.

"Jerk!" Moonbay spat at Daro as the men pulled him away to the edge of the deck. "Remember you are sending yourself to death, because you are just like me and would have done just as I have. It won't be long before you die as stupidly as ...."

"Shut him up," Noga said, who had assumed de facto command.

Someone thrust a dirty rag into Moonbay's mouth. His eyes bulged in a burning glare of accusation at Daro, as the men picked up and hurled him overboard like a sack of grain. The chugging of the engine, the wind, and the waves breaking at the sides did not quite drown the splash.

At the moment, as if nature had conspired to erase Moonbay's memory, the San Pedro happened to be sitting right on top of a large school of sailfish. The men went into feverish work to bring in all they could of this prized fish, not minding the back-breaking toil of hauling in each time several hundred pounds of determined resistance.

As soon as the line came near the surface and the fish smelled air, it broke surface and leaped clear in a graceful curve with the dorsal fins stretched taut like the mainsail of a genoa running before the wind. One, at least ten feet long, leaped vertically, hovered in the air for a breathtaking second or two, then its glistening body, aqua blue and dark on top and dazzling white at the belly, compact like a long-range missile, slick like a girl of thirteen grown to her full height, turned windward with a barely visible jerk of the tail. The long power house of the best fish meat in all the oceans arced, the sword of its head as point, like an acrobat in a dive. So continued the spectacular death struggle of this glorious tribe of fast travelers that respected no boundary, cruising now to the east of the Pacific, now to the west, then the Indian Ocean, the Atlantic.

The eighty-man crew worked round the clock hauling the lines in. By sunset they got to the 200th batch and the photosensitive light buoys began to flash. Night fell quickly at sea, the orange red pulses of light from the buoys providing the only illumination in the total darkness. The work was to go on way past midnight.

"We are in contact with the fleet," said Wonsil Sung, the radio operator, coming up to Daro.

"What do they want?" Daro said, gruff with fatigue.

"They have a man overboard at the Daywang, the flagship," Sung said.

"That's their problem," Daro said. "Anyway talk to Noga about it."

"It's our problem," Sung persisted. "The man overboard is the owner's son, Charley Hyun, you know, the jetsetter who lived in Los Angeles."

"How did he get mixed up in this?"

"They picked him up at San Diego. Apparently he wanted to learn the business from the bottom up before taking over from his old man."

Being the owner's son, he had been given the usual soft treatment, and was allowed to go anywhere in the ship, butting in on any part of the operations. At one point the main line was being hauled in by the winch, pulling up the branch lines out of the water. One of them revealed a big shark on its hook. The attendant stopped the winch and got ready to cut the shark off. Charley asked to take over. Taking the line from the attendant Charley wound it a few times around his fist so it would not slip through. The line slacked as the shark swam along the side of the ship. Charley drew the line in, winding the remaining slack around his forearm. Suddenly the line pulled with a snap as the shark dove down, taking its handler overboard. The body never surfaced. The ship followed the currents, making the best calculations, but had no luck. So the whole fleet had been put to the task of finding the body. The San Pedro was ordered to join the search off the coast of Mexico.

For nine days and nights the ship crisscrossed the ocean with no island or coast in sight to relieve the emptiness, with only tenuous radio contact with the rest of the fleet. On the tenth night blinding search lights blazed through the dark and scanned the San Pedro from stern to bow. Outside the focus of light, as the beams shifted, the crew could make out two coast guard cutters, one on each side of the ship. Men armed with automatic weapons stood in position ready to shoot. A loudspeaker blared in an unintelligible tongue.

"Spanish," one of the crew said.

Another made out the words "El Salvador." The search lights zeroed in on the bridge.

"Viente, Kapitano! Viente, Kapitano!" repeated the loudspeaker.

"Don't look at me," Noga said, petulantly.

"This is the Coast Guard of El Salvador," the microphone crackled in a Spanish-accented English.

How did they fail to notice their approach?

Daro wondered, looking at the radarscope which now accurately showed the blips for the coast guard vessels.

"Stop engine," the order came. "Kapitan, prepare to come aboard. We are closing in."

The cutter on the starboard inched nearer, a dangerous operation in any condition of the sea, but particularly so now with the sea heaving unpredictably. The cutter was only ten feet away.

"Stand by to take the rope," the microphone shrilled.

As the uniformed men with rifles at the ready still kept their alert positions, a group of men stood amidship in the penumbra of the arc light preparing to throw a line across.

"Get the men ready," Daro said, nudging Noga who seemed spellbound.

"Okay, okay," Noga grunted and left the bridge.

Five men were positioned on the deck, eyeing their counterparts on the cutter.

"Fix the rope on top of the bridge," the instructions came along with the rope. The men scrambled up the companionway and onto the roof, tying the rope to the cleat by the flagpole. The cutter eased off and the rope tightened.

"We are standing by," the microphone said. "Captain, come aboard, leaving word with the second in command to follow the coast guard."

As the meaning of the capture sank in, Noga stood, face drained of blood, trembling.

"They must have found out about Moonbay," Noga whispered through paled lips.

"Don't worry," Daro said, putting his hand on Noga's shoulder. "Nothing will happen. Just a routine check."

"Don't get any ideas," Noga said, shaking Daro's hand off. "You were right there from the beginning when it all happened. You are in it just as much as the rest of us."

The sputter of the loudspeaker from the cutter grew more impatient.

"They are asking for you," Daro reminded Noga.

"Why me? Why don't you go and see what they want?"

"Because I am not the captain. They are asking for the captain."

"Neither am I."

"You are the first officer and captain now."

"No, we have no captain, as you know. If we have a captain at all, it is you. You have master's papers and would be in command of a whole fleet if you had not left for America. You must go."

"I don't have the papers with me, nor the uniform."

"Get Moonbay's, in the closet there."

Dead man's clothes and Moonbay's at that! The very idea made his skin crawl.

"Look here!" Noga said, straightening himself. "You say I am the captain. Okay, I am it then. As captain of the ship I am ordering you. Put on the jacket and hat and get going."

With the next blast of the loudspeaker Noga's authoritative stance crumpled to mouse-like cravenness. Daro picked up the captain's jacket, epauletted with gold braids, tasseled at the sleeves and breasted with medals, and the triple gold banded hat from the captain's corner, as it was called, which was perhaps more sacrosanct than where the gyroscope was kept.

"Looks tailor-made for you," Noga said when Daro finished dressing, and would have gone on to make some more witticisms on the subject, but stopped short noticing Daro's glare.

Daro opened the door and stepped into the white light. There was a murmur among the San Pedro crew, some of whom could swear they were seeing things, Moonbay's ghost up and about among them.

The cutter with the hawser across came closer and Daro jumped off the San Pedro, holding on to the line. As soon as he landed on the cutter, armed men surrounded him and poked him with the muzzles of their weapons. A couple of them pushed his hands up, over his head. After a rough frisking of his body they led him to the bridge, where Captain Huarez waited.

"You are in the waters of El Salvador," Huarez said.

"We are in the open sea, at least 150 miles from the coast," Daro said.

"Fifty-four miles to be exact," Huarez said. "Our boundary begins from 200 miles off anyway. That's the law of the seas now."

As navigator Daro had known that they were not too far from the Central American coasts, but his calculations must have been off quite a bit. Astronomical navigation always left a margin of error, but this was a real bummer, being off by a hundred miles. Cloudy nights had hid the sky but that did not mollify his mortification.

"We were not doing anything illegal," Daro said. "We weren't even fishing. We were looking for a dead crewman."

"For ten days?" Huarez said with a smile of superior knowledge. "We have had you under surveillance."

"It's customary with us whenever a man falls overboard," Daro said. "Don't you do the same?"

"Only three days at most. You can't find anything after that in these currents. You must come up with a better explanation than that. Be honest. You were spying, weren't you?"

"Search our ship. What possible interest could we have in spying on your country? We are Koreans. The boat is a Korean fishing vessel, a deep sea albacoreman."

"Is San Pedro a Korean name? You don't have to lie. The ship is Soviet-built, commissioned by Nicaragua, our unfriendly neighbor. I have documentary evidence right here."

Huarez tapped a clipboard.

"Doesn't it say that the ship was bought by the Mitsubishi Marines of Japan and was subsequently leased to the Korean firm Daywang Fisheries? I have the papers in my cabin. A call to the Mitsubishi will confirm my story."

The interrogation, reiterative and irrelevant, seemed endless.

The black sky broke into a million forked tongues, one deafening thunder following another. The sharp blue of lightning numbed the retina. Rain drops the size of pebbles boiled the sea and pelted the steel hull making the noise of a thousand drums struck at once. However, what astounded Daro was that this violent eructation of nature did not seem to faze any of the crew, who went about their routine as if only a breeze was passing by.

"It happens every day at this time," one of them

explained but this did not reassure Daro who peered anxiously into the dark for the San Pedro. The lightning seemed to have shorted out the lights. He could not see the required blue and red lights on its sides. Only the lights of the other cutter could be seen intermittently in the distance, between flashes of lightning.

The door of the cabin in which Daro had been locked banged open. Commander Huarez walked in, followed by his lieutenants.

"Where is your boat?" Huarez said.

"Isn't it behind us?" Daro said, craning his head.

A sharp slap on his face rattled him. The welts on the cheek burned and instinctively his hand went up to feel the hurt. Another slap on the other cheek was accompanied by a command to keep still.

"No lights. No trace of it in the radarscope. The sonofabitch has given us the slip," Huarez said. "Are you really the captain of the boat?"

There was just the briefest hesitation as Daro debated whether it might not be wise to come right out and confess to the small deception he had been forced to practice. These people might understand what it meant to be under orders and free him as guiltless. Free him in the middle of the ocean? Their fierce looks and the ever-present proximity of physical violence convinced him that they would sooner throw him overboard to save themselves embarrassment, if he were a nonentity.

"I am the captain," Daro said.

"Then prove it by calling your ship back," Huarez said.

"Okay, let me try."

He was taken to the radio room next to the bridge.

"Give the operator your frequency."

"Try 780 megacycles," Daro said to a uniformed officer before the console.

The operator repeated the call signs but there was no reply. Daro took the microphone himself and called Noga, called him all kinds of names for slinking away like that, leaving him in the lurch. After haranguing at some length, convincingly, he put down the microphone in disgust.

"Traitors, mutineers," Daro said in genuine anger. "Help me get to the first port and report it to the authorities, so I can punish these pirates who stole my ship."

The captain and his associates talked in Spanish, occasionally throwing suspicious glances at Daro.

"Let's go after them," Daro said. "Captain Huarez, I think I know where they went. Turn 120 degrees. The ship must have headed for Nicaragua where we have our agent."

"We can't," Huarez said. "We are not on friendly terms with Nicaragua, as I told you, and our hot pursuit will be interpreted as invasion of territory."

Acajutla was a good-sized bay, ideal as a port, but what piers there were had been taken over by naval craft of all sorts, including a few destroyers. It was El Salvador's naval base for its Pacific fleet, the coast guard being an ancillary unit. Only a small section was used by local fishermen, mostly trawlers.

As soon as the cutter docked, Daro was taken to a waiting jeep and driven to the Navy Headquarters, an imposing structure of stone in contrast to the squalor of the homes and shops. Later Daro was to find the splendor of the living quarters for the officers matching that of their offices. Built Spanish-style, with colonnades and arches, the district commander's mansion on the brow of a wooded hill overlooking the countryside and the sea was a beautiful castle of ageless grace and beauty from a distance, but upon closer view armed guards patrolled every inch of the grounds like a fortress.

A Navy captain, clean shaven, dark skinned, of Spanish descent, sat at a fiberglass-topped mahogany desk, studying the report on Daro.

"When were you in Nicaragua?" Captain Mendoza asked.

"I have not been to Nicaragua," Daro said.

"What is your rank in the North Korean navy?"

"I am a South Korean."

Daro decided to keep quiet about his permanent resident status in the US. The US consul wouldn't be able to help him, as he was not a citizen, and his immigration status would only complicate things, the relationship between El Salvador and the US being on the touchy side lately, with increasing US criticism of the repressive Salvadoran regime.

"Show me your passport."

"It is on my ship."

"Why don't you carry it around on you?"

"I have all my important documents locked up in the safe aboard my ship. Like your people I had assumed my boat was close behind."

"We can shoot you as an infiltrator and spy without trial."

Armed guards pushed him out of the intelligence chief's office. The captain's uniform was taken away from Daro, and an ill-fitting, foul-smelling prison garb thrown at him. The lockup, with bare walls and unswept floor, was an oven during the day and a freezer at night. There was no bed to sleep on, no bedroll to crawl into.

Unable to lie on the floor or lean against the concrete wall, Daro paced the room and rubbed himself to keep warm through the interminable night before succumbing to fitful sleep, folded up in a corner.

"By condemning me you have written your own death warrant, because you are me."

Daro jumped to his feet, Moonbay's shouts still ringing in his ear. The guard, who had kicked him awake, told him to strip for morning washup. It was still dark except for a faint glow in the east. Shivering, he was marched with other naked men into a yard where on signal the guards turned water hoses on them. The jet streams seemed to bore holes in their skin rather than clean them up, but this bizarre version of public bath apparently fortified the conviction of the Salvadoran authorities that they ran a perfectly sanitary and humane prison and justified in their view the continual wear and bequeathal of the same clothes from one prisoner to the next, unlaundered.

The unchanging diet, meal after meal, of stone hard tortilla and water thin catfish soup, was unbearable. Other prisoners had homemade food brought by their families, the aroma of which made him dizzy with longing.

He was paraded through the town at the head of marching columns, a Navy band leading the way. The populace had turned out in force. There must be precious little else going on by way of public entertainment. The sailors, smart-stepping to some crude brass band music with an Oriental prisoner as their prize, was enough of a novelty for the crowds to come from miles around on foot. They jostled and jockeyed for vantage points. Daro almost wished he were a monster, with three eyes and five arms maybe, not to disappoint them. Nevertheless he was quite a hit and they goggled at him with intense curiosity.

From the other cells, tenanted by Salvadorans, issued hideous screams and groans at all hours, setting his teeth on edge. Now and then he saw through the peep hole bloodied and broken bodies being carried out past his door like slaughtered carcass. Every time the boots of the guards rang in the hall he froze and braced for his turn. The hopelessness of his case became increasingly more evident. He would die like a nameless caged lab animal at the pleasure of these sadists and butchers, and nobody would be the wiser. Life began like a spark in the darkness. With some the spark glowed and flashed, however briefly, spreading its brightness from horizon to horizon, but with him it fizzled out, without so much as a sputter, unnoticed, unmissed. The pity of it brought tears to his eyes. What was the next world like? Was it to be just an extension of earthly existence with all its invidious inequality or was it to be a true republic where every soul was equal, where luck had no role because it was luck that created all that unfairness, injustice, disparity? He would find it one or the other soon enough.

"You still maintain your name is Daro Jo?" a younger interrogator asked him for the umpteenth time.

"Yes, I am Daro Jo."

"We have checked the Korean addresses you have put down but nobody has heard about you."

"They are my land addresses for documentary purposes, but I have hardly lived at any of them. Like you I am a sailor and have spent most of my life at sea."

"You have no relatives?"

"No, my parents died during the Korean War and most of my relatives would have nothing to do with me."

"The name Moonbay Sin doesn't mean anything to you?"

Oh, that horrible name again! Couldn't it be blotted out as its bearer had been? Or must it hound him to his death?

"No," Daro said biting his lips.

The junior officer looked at him quizzically,

then raised his hand and twirled his index finger at his head before leaving the room with a grin.

"I am Dr. Coronado, a psychiatrist," the next investigator introduced himself.

"What is this?" Daro cried. "There is nothing wrong with my head. Ask me any question. I can do differential calculus. Have you heard of Taylor's Theorem, my dear doctor?"

"Some of the smartest men can become the victims of temporary mental lapse or delusion. You have been under tremendous stress, enough to unsettle any man...."

"Get out of here!" Daro lost his temper as he never had and let fly a punch at the doctor's jaw.

Back at his cell Daro expected dire retribution momentarily. Instead the turnkey opened the door with a woman in tow, one Emelda Agapito, dark-complexioned, half Spanish, half Indian, in her thirties, maybe forties, medium build, huge brown eyes, hollow cheeks, almost ghostly, a shawl over her head.

"The wild man is all yours," he said to her, closing the door. "Don't be too long. We need his space."

"Moonbay!" she screamed, throwing her arms around him.

"Moonbay Sin?" Daro echoed the name, incredulously.

"Yes, Moonbay! I've missed you so much all this time. But I've never stopped praying for your return. God has heard my prayers. I'll burn fifty candles to the Virgin. We'll never part again."

So the wretch had been there, sowing his wild oats!

"Signorina!"

"I couldn't believe my eyes when I saw your picture in the papers. You haven't changed a bit, though thinned. The food here must have been awful. I'll fatten you up back to your old self in no time."

"I don't know you. I am not the man you take me for. My name is Daro Jo."

"Let's not talk about it, not just yet," she said, bursting into laughter, high-pitched peals, clear like chimes, which sent cold shivers down his back.

There was no undeceiving Emelda, who took his denials as some kind of elaborate game he had devised for her amusement.

"Perhaps you are a North Korean spy after all as the papers say," she said indulgently. "Of course I don't give a damn whether you are a communist or not. Politics is rubbish anyway. Nothing matters so long as we are back together."

Daro listened mesmerized to this amazing narrative being woven about him like a cocoon around a pupa.

"Who do you think put the Navy doctor up to your diagnosis of amnesia?"

Daro shook his head dumbly.

"Me," she said, jabbing at her breast triumphantly. "I've paid him enough money to buy himself a new car, maybe even a new house, the son of a bitch. So you don't have to pretend with me. Now pay attention. Even if you are amnesiac, I have some things that will bring back your memory in a flash."

She spread out before him two photographs of her and Moonbay. One had Moonbay sitting on a rock that overlooked a bay. He was looking directly into the camera, serene and alert, like a lion guarding his pride.

"You are so handsome," she mussed his hair and kissed him before turning to the second picture. In swim suits they were running up the sandy slope of a beach, with a gigantic surf curled and poised to strike from behind.

"Don't you remember I almost drowned and you had to pull me out of the undertow?" she asked, her grateful eyes moist.

Daro again shook his head.

"This is going too far," she said, frowning, unable to hide her annoyance. "These pictures are hard evidence even the Salvadoran authorities couldn't help accepting. Nobody is being fooled. So you may as well drop the pretense. Here, put on your uniform and let's get the hell out of here."

Unwrapping a bundle, she disclosed Moonbay's uniform, washed and ironed. They must have released it to her custody. She fingered the second button from the top, and pushed it to one side, revealing yellow nylon thread holding it down to the black serge.

"Look at this!" she exclaimed. "I didn't have any black thread to match and had to use the yellow. Do you still deny you are Moonbay?"

Daro stared stupidly at the button and the yellow thread under it, an inverted U of a dozen strands looped around the eye of the button. By a curious optic illusion each strand magnified to the size of a main-line rope, then writhed and coiled about him into the shape of a noose. He shook his head to dispel the vision.

"I don't know what all this masquerade is about," Emelda went on. "I don't care. The important thing is that you've returned to me, Emelda, your destiny, as you called me. You promised to return, to be mine forever and never leave my side again. You have returned. We'll get the best lawyer money can buy. It's all your money, our money. I've invested the money you gave me wisely. The bar is a success. We're rich.

We can sell everything and go live anywhere in the world...."

Listening to the torrent of fairy tale, Daro was powerless to correct the mistaken identity. She would not cease calling him Moonbay until he nodded and answered to the name. So absolute and unshakable was her conviction that he caught himself thinking perhaps he was really Moonbay. Anyway, one phone call to the Korean Embassy would clear up everything. They must all know her to be insane. Why bother to prove gravity, the existence of the elements, the roundness of the earth?

A soothing, haunting Latin tune, the thin wail of a high male falsetto, wafted through the night air.

"Moonbay! Moonbay!" Emelda shouted, her work-coarsened body writhing and exploding in tumultuous love-making.

"Yes! Yes!" Daro nodded.

Emelda rose, went to a drawer, and came back holding some object behind her naked body.

"Guess what!" she said.

"I give up," Daro said, yawning.

With celerity and violence that made him jump she thrust a pistol in the pit of his stomach. Daro winced.

"This is the revolver you gave me to swear our

faith by," Emelda said.

Made of silver, it shone, ornate, small as her palm but deadly. His whole body spasmed. The joke had gone too far. He should have a serious talk with her.

"Emelda!" Daro began, taking a deep breath.

"I am so glad you've kept your word and come back," she said. "You know of course that I have kept my part of our bargain. I would have shot any man who would compromise me. I would have shot myself if I had been untrue to you. Whoever breaks our oath was to end his or her shameful life with this, remember?"

She spun the cylinder expertly and the chambers, loaded with tiny bullets, clicked away in mortal accents.

"You'll never go away now," she continued with her breathless litany. "We'll be happy forever. You are mine forever...."

There was no talking sense to her. It would have to wait.

She insisted on coming with him to San Salvador.

"What about the bar?" Daro protested.

"My staff will look after it," Emelda replied.

"I have things to take care of at the Korean Embassy."

"Where the needle goes, the thread goes. That's

our saying for...."

Damn! he muttered under his breath, the vision of the yellow noose floating back to his mind.

At San Salvador he persuaded her with difficulty to wait at a hotel while he went to present himself to the ambassador. At the Embassy he was instantly recognized by the receptionist without his announcing himself and was shown directly to the office of Ambassador Wonho Lim, a balding rotund man who came from his desk and warmly grasped Daro's hands.

"I am honored to meet the national hero," Lim said.

"National hero, sir?" Daro asked bewildered.

"Yes. You are a celebrity. But of course you don't know anything about it. Stupid of me to forget you have been incommunicado all this time. We got nowhere with the Salvadorans who stonewalled, denied all knowledge of your whereabouts."

He rang and a secretary brought in a pile of Korean newspapers. The captions and articles raved about a brave man who risked his own life to save his ship San Pedro. By a unanimous vote the Korean National Assembly had awarded him the Hibiscus Medal, the highest peace time honor, to express his country's gratitude for preventing the loss of millions of dollars. Page after page carried Moonbay's pictures, the hero who took on and scattered single-handed the whole Salvadoran coast guard. Nowhere was Daro Jo, the real hero of the piece, even mentioned.

"But these are not my pictures," Daro stammered.

Puzzled, Lim looked from him to the pictures, then broke into a smile.

"Do I detect a touch of Narcissism here? Newsprint cannot do full justice to your handsome features."

"No, it's not what you think. The truth of the matter is...."

The secretary came in and put a tray of papers and letters on Lim's desk.

"This is your new passport and ID," Lim said.

Daro gasped, looking wide-eyed at the passport photo, another resurrection of Moonbay. How clever of them to write Daro off so they wouldn't have to account for a missing body! It must have been that snake Noga's idea. How was he, Daro Jo, to prove his identity, his existence? Could he overturn the weight of accumulated counter-evidence? To what purpose should he?

Among the mail was a letter of appreciation from the Daywang Fisheries for restoring the San Pedro to the mother fleet, which was off to the coast of Chile for alba core. He, Moonbay Sin, was offered captaincy of the company's latest acquisition, the 7,000-ton factory ship Sun. Enclosed was a check for $10,000 and a first-class airplane ticket to Honolulu, where the fleet was to meet him on his way to Samoa. In the meantime he was on his own, and could charge everything to the company.   "Come to the party tonight," Lim said. "In honor of the musical group, the Melodies of Korea, but now in honor of you. After what you've been through you can use some recreation. They've had an enthusiastic reception everywhere they went, France, Germany, England, USA. Their stop here is mainly to take it easy and rest up, though I can't imagine why they should choose an out-of-the-way place like this for a vacation spot. The group leader is Hayran Sohn. You've heard of her?"

"Heard of her! I used to buy every record of hers. What time did you say it was?"

"Six p.m."

"I need a hair cut, a bath, and a suit...."

"I hope you have no objections to my reserving a suite at the Waldorf San Salvador. That's where the musicians are staying, too. The hotel has the best tailor, barbershop, haberdashery, you name it."

Basking in the easy conversation around the table, laden with barbecued short ribs of beef, corvena, raw fillets of tuna, assorted mountain herbs, and kimchee, seasoned and flavored in a way that stirred and penetrated to the innermost recesses of his being, Daro couldn't help smiling at Emelda's efforts to impress him with her nation's culinary resources. Unalterably, ineluctably, he was Korean, couldn't be anything but Korean, he told himself, content with the discovery.

Daro was distinctly conscious of Hayran's interest in him. A child prodigy since she was seven and with dozens of hit records to her credit, she lacked nothing, neither money nor fawning men. In her early forties, she had never married, preferring to have one liaison after another. Her last reported affair was with Hwajin Min, head of an engineering and construction conglomerate doing multi-billion-dollar business in Saudi Arabia. Could it be that a woman like her reaches a saturation point with successful men and retrogrades to common types like himself? Or perhaps he was not all that common after all. There was always that aura of adventure and romance with which the landsmen's imagination cloaked the lowliest sailor. In his case he was a captain of some distinction, what with the Hibiscus Medal and all, which he had indeed earned, though in the name of his hated enemy by force of unavoidable circumstances.

"So we hear you have this crazy native woman hanging around your neck like an incubus," observed Hongyon Hwang, the group's director. "But I don't see that as an affliction. Not at all. I would welcome such rich incubi anytime."

The Embassy had confirmed that Emelda Agapito was as good as her word, sole owner of the Latin Palace in Acajutla.

"How fascinating!" Hayran said.

"I swear I've never seen this woman before in my life," Daro felt a sudden urge to make a clean breast of the whole mess to this singing star.

"Love at first sight," she said, voice subdued, lambent eyes burrowing into his.

"It's all a case of mistaken identity. She takes me for somebody else."

"There is no such thing as mistaken identity. You are right there in front of her to see and touch and she takes you for what you are."

"But to be called by somebody else's name...."

"What is there to a name?" Hayran said. "The real person under the label, the veneer, is what we should be concerned with."

"Like under the sheet?" observed Miryo Han, a vivacious alto in her twenties, giggling.

The whole table rocked with merriment. The joke had been presumably at Hayran's expense but she laughed harder than anybody else and nobody remembered what the joke had been about as they kept laughing, doubling over. Meeting Hayran's desire-filled eyes Daro felt reassured. Uncannily she seemed to read his mind. He had every right to her attentions. As she said, he was there, the real Daro Jo, in person, for her to ogle at and feel aroused by. He wasn't deceiving anybody, had no false pretenses. Only if life were decided on such terms, on real terms. As it was, the dice fell every which way. The most trivial, infinitesimal difference, a few points more or less in the exam score, a few dollars more or less than the next lowest bid, gall, bluff, cheek, above all dumb luck or chance, failed or promoted a man's cause.

"Speaking as local authority," Ambassador Lim said in mock furtiveness, looking in the direction of the kitchen where his wife had gone to oversee the next course, "Salvadoran women are tigers in love."

"They bite and scratch?" inquired Pilsoo Ham, the deadpan changgo drummer.

This triggered another round of laughter, after which nobody remembered anything about El Salvador or its women. They moved on, with interruptions of laughter, from one topic to another, about people and things they had seen in Paris, London, Rome, Chicago, Tokyo.

It was in the cards that Hayran should ask Daro to her suite after they had arrived at the Waldorf from the Embassy party to listen to her tapes, especially since he had been away from home so long. From the 43rd floor the panorama was incomparable - lighted avenues, buildings, parks, lofty Mount San Salvador dominating the skyline to the west, Lake Ilopango gleaming like a mirror to the east, the countryside marching somberly to the edge of the Pacific. The stars, eclipsed by the moon, twinkled shyly and a cool, crisp breeze, unique to the high altitude of these tropics, rustled the partially drawn curtains.

"Better than air conditioning as the tourist flyer says," Hayran said.

"Yes, it's really pleasant," Daro agreed.

He was soon transported on the wings of lilting tunes, the Bird Song, Cape Changsan, the Boat of No Return, in her mellow, dark soprano, aching with sorrow and yearning under the guise of levity and detachment, the strange mixture of joy and despondency that was uniquely Korean.

Moved to tears he beheld the blurred figure of Hayran standing by the window, her sky-blue jacket with striped sleeves shimmering, the epitome of Korean womanhood, of all womanhood.

His many months of loneliness culminated in

their embrace, which was his restoration to his native element, reaffirming his true identity. Grateful, relieved that it hadn't been too late, he felt like the prodigal son returned to his parental home. A flood of emotions choked him as he felt her reciprocating warmth, arms tightening around him like tendrils, silky fragrant black hair under his nose, taut nipples against his chest, lithe body undulating in unison.

Vaguely he had heard a door crashing open and a distant cry, probably punctuating Hayran's orgasm. There had been a glint of silver, but that could have been the key to the heaven of unmixed bliss he had heard about as he grew up.

Daro never regained consciousness as he faded into nothingness.

THE FOE

Flying over Sangtuc Valley near the Laotian border where G-2 had reported a concentration of Vietcong regulars, the men in the chopper sat rigid, alert for any noise above the drone of the propellers. Lt. John Kim hated these rides. Though the craft looked sturdy close up, its aluminum body hard against his knuckles, it was as vulnerable as a balloon. It might climb vertically, plummet, wiggle, scuttle, and execute many fancy maneuvers, but up there in the sky it was still a sitting duck. The men in the chopper, totally at the mercy of the ground snipers, could only hold their breath and wait helplessly for the fatal blow. John had opted for jungle duty precisely to avoid this, but in Vietnam one ended up in a helicopter no matter what his tactical classification. The Vietcong hideouts were simply inaccessible by other means of transportation.

Of course the jungle had its risks - poisonous snakes, six-inch-long leeches, mosquitoes, booby traps, and the cunning Vietcong themselves, dedicated fighters with spears, daggers, Soviet-made rifles, grenades, and rockets. Nevertheless, he had a fighting chance in the jungle, where he could melt into the familiar element. The Vietcong couldn't be any more elusive or deadly than the tusked boars of Kahaluu, cunning and lightning fast, which he had hunted with his father. But he would do anything to get away from the limbo of the chopper's belly.

Involuntarily John turned to look at Lt. Paul Singer, the pilot. How could he stand it day in and day out? But apparently he did, very well, and thrived on it, surviving a dozen crashes - one of which had involved John.

Caught in a Vietcong ambush, every member of John's nine-man patrol had to fend for himself. Once separated from his men, John could not reconnect. Blindly he ran for cover but bullets followed him everywhere, forcing him down. The moment he raised his head an inch or made any move, a burst of bullets pinned him down again. He could feel the stealthy steps in the dark, closing in for the kill.

Out of nowhere a chopper buzzed overhead, blasting away at the Vietcong. They turned their attention to the new target, shelling it into a sieve. Undaunted, the chopper kept up its counter fire, deliberately seeking the enemy. The pilot had no reason to expose himself and his machine to such overwhelming odds. Nobody would have faulted his loyalty or courage if he had beat a retreat at that point. But he hung on, returning bullet for bullet, drawing the fire to himself. Then a slammer got the chopper in the forward section.

The engine gurgled dead and the craft exploded into a fireball.

"The poor guy!" John said to himself, smitten with guilt and gratitude as he watched the fire smolder away. He had scrambled to higher ground during the diversion.

Startled by a swish near him, John almost squeezed the trigger when Paul's voice stopped him in time. After parachuting out just prior to the explosion, Paul had found his way to the hill, guided by John's transponder. Soon several choppers converged on the area, blocking further pursuit by the Vietcong.

The red warning light flashed. In sixty seconds it would turn green and the exit door slide open. The men would jump off the chopper at four-second intervals with clock-like precision to prevent a pileup on the ground. Trustingly, they would plunge into the black abyss of the night, as if it were some warm pool, though it might very well be the last impression of the earth they would ever get. Looking them over, John felt his heart swell with pride - professionals barely out of their teens, prematurely aged by the war, wearing their 100-pound chutes and backpacks like tailor-made suits.

Paul turned around in his seat and flashed a big dimpled smile. John reciprocated, pushing his thumb up. Forty more seconds to go! John could already feel the rushing wind caress his skin like the waves off Waikiki. In the brief seconds of freefall he was floating on his back in the Pacific, staring into the night sky, the sea lapping around his ears and murmuring a thousand endearments. His friends had told him he was crazy to swim at night, when the sharks closed in from the deep for their nightly feeding. Occasionally the fear had gripped him, especially when some detached seaweed or floating debris nudged at him, but he had grown used to it.

John's first jump had been from a C-135, the regular paratroop carrier. He had been freefalling for at least ten seconds. The gravity-sensitive button would open the chute at the right altitude automatically. He did not have to worry about counting the seconds and hitting the button as with the old models. What if the gadget did not function? The only way to find out before it was too late was to check the length of descent against the jump-off altitude; he could hit the manual button if the chute didn't open at 2,000 feet. How many seconds did that give him? The jump-off altitude was 18,000 feet. Exactly twenty three seconds to freefall 16,000 feet. But he had forgotten to keep track of the time. How could he have been so stupid? Was that unlikely event happening to him, the failure of the automatic pressure button? He pressed the backup button and pulled hard at the cords, wondering whether the chute would respond in time. It opened instantly, jolting him, changing the pitch of the wind gusting by. He hit the ground hard but was unhurt. Did the automatic button work properly and he panic for nothing? Even after many jumps he still could not answer with certainty. In any case the scare had been real enough and never left him. Particularly disturbing was the recurring image of himself being skewered on a tree limb like a shish-kebab.

The green light was just flicking on when the barrage came. Inch-thick bullets ripped through the fuselage, smashing the top propellers and sending the chopper into a tailspin. The pilots struggled with the steering wheel, kicked at the levers, and madly activated the emergency controls, but the ship spun and spun, tossing the men about. Then came the crash.

John regained consciousness, coughing with the smoke, gagging in the heat wave, the crackle of fire all around him. Scattered about him were broken, twisted, bleeding bodies. Death must have been instantaneous. Not a hand twitched. Sgt.

Dan Simpson, an explosives expert from Bowling Green, Ohio, lay nearby, his back turned to him as if he were asleep. John turned him over. The open eyes stared lifeless. Kicking the tangle of bodies off, John made his way to the cockpit. Paul's head was stuck in the steel-reinforced bullet-proof windshield. His face, raked by the jagged teeth of the broken glass, was a bloody mess. The copilot was crushed between his seat and the trap bent inward.

Waving the flames aside, John dashed to the midsection, yanked the hatchet off the wall, and hacked away at the door, but the buckled jamb held the door locked tight. Leaping back to the front, John swung the hatchet at the windshield around the pilots head to widen the opening. The hatchet slipped in his sweaty palms and struck the skull, splitting it with a sickening crunch. Wiping the blood that spattered his face, he tried in vain to pry the head out of the opening, stuck as in a vise. The flames began licking at his boots. John lifted the hatchet and struck the neck. The hatchet sank deep, parting the neckbone, but head and thorax held together by skin and tendon. Six more strokes were necessary to effect a clean cut. John pushed the slumped torso off the panel, then kicked Paul's head out, clearing the opening. The flames were already singeing his hair. Desperately John widened the opening with the hatchet, knocking the glass off and bending the wire mesh out. He squeezed through and jumped off the burning craft, and was greeted by a burst of bullets. No sooner had he ducked, zigzagged and dived behind a clump of brush than a barrage of bullets cut it down to the ground as neatly as grass under a lawn mower. Exposed, John ran, flopped to the ground, rolled over, and crawled behind a rock. Stone chips stung his face and puffs of dust filled his nose, leaving bitter grit in his mouth. The explosion of the helicopter drove him further into the ground. The dull glaze of the mushrooming fire made his bloody hands and clothes seem even bloodier.

Something dangled in his left hand. Paul's gold necklace with his dogtag and cross, blood-soaked, bits of chopped flesh and bone stuck in the links. A sudden surge of fury sent John to his feet. No longer hearing the screech of projectiles flying at him he ran screaming, blasting away with his M-16 toward the spot where the fiercest barrage was coming from. With every change in the direction of fire he turned and ran to it like an indestructible machine, emptying clip after clip. When his ammunition was gone, he hurled the grenades three or four at a time. When they were gone, he fixed the bayonet to his rifle and thrust at the shrubbery, behind trees and rocks. After nearly an hour of lunging and stabbing, he noticed that the area was quiet. Either the fire at the wreckage had burned out or he had moved far enough away from it so he couldn't see. The Vietnam night was so thick that he could almost grasp it.

He stalked after any rustle or creak in the jungle, determined to rub out Vietcong vermin from the face of the earth. He stumbled into a bubbling stream, ankle deep. Carefully he waded across, trying not to disturb the gravel or the music of the water. The bank rose steeply before him. Waist-high reeds and grass sighed and insects chirped mutedly.

Vaulting up the ridge, he came up against a black shape, a Vietcong, judging from the small, slouched silhouette. The point of a bayonet poked at his breast. Though his entire body froze, by reflex he raised his bayonet to the Vietcong's chest. An eternity passed before his blood recirculated and his senses functioned again.

"Amerikang!" whispered the Vietcong.

In the heightened perception of the moment, John felt the man's pulse, sweat, and smell. Perhaps this was a young farmer whose wife and child had been killed in a bombardment, who had been run out his home and farm, who had gone to school and learned classical Chinese, French, and math.

"Vietcong!" John replied. As if by mutual accord they relaxed the pressure on their bayonets, then slowly backed away, a step at a time, until the darkness swallowed them up.

THE GARDENER

I thought Pang lived somewhere in Kalihi, probably at the Linapuni government housing, and was about to take the Punahou ramp into the freeway when he asked me, since I was so kind as to drive him, to go straight and take him to the Renaissance. I couldn't picture him as a patron of the night club and pulled up at the rear parking lot in some mystery. A woman in her early thirties, dark eyes sparkling under long lashes, darted out of the back door and went to the passenger side.

"Father, I was about to send Chulsoon," she said, balancing an umbrella over him against the gusting wind.

So his daughter was no less than Miyon, the proprietor of the Renaissance. I felt as if I had been under observation all along.

"I am no exploiter," I protested inwardly.

One hundred dollars a month was the most I could spare for gardening and, as a matter of fact, I had not intended to continue spending it as long as I had. I could have terminated after, say, six months, after the first face lift, since our agreement provided that either party could call off any time. He could budget his time to suit himself and I expected him to come about once a week with a lawnmower and shears. But he came almost every day, spending the whole day to dig out the roots of nutgrass and nettle. Only when they got quite broken, he began to take shorter hours and take some days off. The place was a marvel with flowers and fruits and we were grateful. For Christmas my wife Muriel spent a morning buying a complete aloha outfit, as well as two sets of Levi pants and tops to replace his eternal military discards.

Through Muriel's connections we found out that Pang kept working, although Miyon was more than willing and capable of taking care of him. He had a few other clients with arrangements similar to ours, besides taking care of Miyon's yard and house at Pacific Heights, where he lived in a basement room.

I was busy the next week or so and didn't see him, as I left the house before he came and returned after he left. Arriving home one Friday evening with a ravenous appetite, I was surprised to find him still working on the roses at the corner of the front lawn. Muriel came out to the balcony, gesturing that the dinner was ready. I was anxious to get in and wash up after greeting Pang, but felt it discourteous to do so. Fully expecting him to refuse, as he had declined all our previous offers of like nature, I invited him to come upstairs and have dinner with us, ignoring a frown on Muriel's face.

"Would it be all right to impose?" he said.

"Nonsense. There won't be anything special,

just a plain ordinary family supper," I said, half for the benefit of my wife who was still on the balcony to ascertain the issue.

"Thank you very much, sir. I will be up in a minute."

Pang came in holding a quart bottle of Chivas Regal. A fifth of what I paid him a month! I told him I would not think of accepting it, but he said it cost him nothing because he took it from his daughter's cellar. We had to acquiesce. Muriel filled his soup bowl first. Our eyes were riveted to his right hand: the fingers had been cut off in the middle, the blunt ends forming an even row across. None of us had ever noticed it before.

"How did you get that?" blurted Willy, my eight-year-old son, in his broken Korean, despite Muriel's severe looks and his sister's nudges.

"I'll tell you all about it," Pang said, giving his hand to Willy and Betty to feel and ogle at to their hearts' content. "But do you understand Korean?"

"Arayo(I understand)!" blustered Willy, at which we all laughed.

After supper, as Muriel washed dishes, folded clothes, and went about the rest of her interminable housework, I asked him to my study to view some Korean scrolls. It was hard to send him or take him home directly after the meal, although I was a little tired and could use some rest. The children were glued to the TV. As soon as we were alone, he said he had a favor to ask of me. Anything, I said.

"It concerns my children," he said.

"Oh, you have more than one, besides the daughter running the Renaissance."

He hesitated a moment.

"I have never told this to anybody, not even to Miyon. You are the only person to know."

I felt a little uncomfortable at this distinction but assured him of my confidentiality.

"You see I have and don't have children," he resumed.

The paradox was pointless but I could see that it wasn't meant to be humorous.

"The daughter I have here is not really my daughter."

"But it's through her that you came to the US, isn't it?"

Like most first-generation immigrants with the obligation to engineer the subsequent influx of all their kinsmen, I knew quite a bit about the US laws on immigration and naturalization.

"Yes. Legally she is my daughter, but there is no blood relationship at all."

"What about the others?" I asked after a pause. "Are they your real children?"

"There is only one, a boy, but I never married

his mother and he bears a different name, Ho, because his mother was married to Byongwon Ho."

Was it a case of adultery or premarital indiscretion? With that clean, childlike face of his?

"Well, this sort of thing happens everywhere. In this culture they have a saying, Lucky is the man who knows his father. But you were married to Miyon's mother, weren't you?"

"I wasn't married to her, either."

"Then you adopted Miyon."

"No, I had to report her as my daughter and her mother as my wife during the refugee years at Pusan."

      •   •   •

He proceeded to give his incredible life history, which began with his freshman year at a college in Seoul. His family firmly believed in his getting an education although their fortunes had declined and the father had to hire himself out as an indentured farmhand to Byongwon Ho, the wealthiest landowner in the village of Woramni, about forty miles southeast of Seoul.

During the summer vacation he came home, walking the whole distance on an empty stomach because he had no money to buy a meal. By the time he began climbing the tortuous path to Roof

Pass, the last formidable obstacle isolating his native village from the outside world, he was ready to collapse with exhaustion. When he reached the top, the sun was sinking behind the mountains. A swirling mist overhung the valley to the peaks. The lower slopes swept down to the green rice paddies, the narrow Willow Creek winding and shimmering in the receding sunlight. Little houses strung out along the edge of the paddies, with vegetable patches valiantly creeping up the hostile mountains, until the incline became vertical and sheer bluffs of gigantic rock blocked further inroads.

Pang got a job as assistant to the village herb doctor, Yoo, whose only daughter Yongshil was engaged to be married to Byongwon Ho, a big man with a savage mien and a matching disposition, a terror to all his farmhands and neighbors. One tenant farmer was crippled for life when discovered underpacking rice sacks to be delivered to Ho in payment for some old debt. Another farmer was pushed off a cliff and was seriously hurt, becoming bedridden for a good part of a year: hired as a beater for a boar hunt, he had committed the indiscretion of taking a circuitous path to avoid a dangerous terrain, thereby leaving a gap in his sector and letting the boar escape. Yongshil was the prettiest girl in the village and the brightest, graduating the top of her class at Mamyongni Elementary. Ho, who had preferred his wild bachelor ways to marriage, had one look at her and asked for her hand. Yoo saw the advantage of the alliance and gave his consent with alacrity, but the girl didn't want it at all. His reputation frightened her. His exploits of brute strength horrified her. The prospect of living with him was like being caged with a tiger for the rest of her life. Though Ho wanted to wed her instantly, which her father found agreeable, she procrastinated, giving as her excuse a decent period of mourning for her recently deceased mother.

Her father's assistant Pang was a slim youth with a delicate face like that of a girl. Courteous, soft-spoken, and a lover of poetry and novels, he talked to her as a friend, as if she was just another boy, sharing her unfulfilled ambitions of studying in Seoul or abroad and becoming a woman scientist. Pang saw nothing unusual about this and encouraged her to order books on mathematics, physics, biology, and chemistry, and study them on her own. Since her father thought any education for women was a luxury, Pang acted as her agent in her scholarly adventure. He walked the fifteen miles to Hwasan Town, the county seat with a high school, to get the books, and they studied them together, avoiding the eye of the disapproving world. They sought out secret places and often went to the hill behind the village. One day it got dark when they started coming down. Yongshil slipped and Pang helped her up, overcoming the physical shyness. They came down the path, holding hands, and reluctantly parted, bidding goodbye till the next day. Thereafter their meetings were no longer purely academic and they contemplated ways of breaking her engagement. Their ultimate solution was elopement, a decision hastened by her pregnancy. She waited for him at the appointed place, but he did not show up even after midnight. The creeping darkness with its myriad noises and illusions frightened her, but she waited and waited, thinking that he was packing his last bag or taking care of some last-minute errand. The half moon dipped behind White Snow Peak and the hootings and squeaks of night creatures quieted to a predawn stillness. Yongshil realized that it was useless to wait any longer and went down the hill to the village. She had to go past Ho's house. Its arched front gate flew open and a group of men, led by Ho, came to her.

"Where were you all night?" asked Ho sharply, his eyes rolling menacingly.

Growing proud in disappointment, she scorned him and felt an urge to boast that she had been with her lover all night and would never marry a bully like Ho.

"Did you get lost while returning from your mother's grave?" her father asked the leading question, stepping forward from behind his future son-in-law.

She remembered the excuses she had given him for her late excursions. His stooped figure, with fear and entreaty written on his face, quelled her defiance.

"I mistook the way by Moon Gully," she said.

"We checked around there," Ho said.

"In the darkness I missed the landmark, the rock pile, and took my turn too early."

"Into Skeleton Gulch?"

She nodded. "I discovered my error half way down and retraced my steps."

Far from satisfied, Ho decided that the engagement should come to a speedy conclusion. They were married a few days afterwards. She yielded to this course though aware of its disastrous potential. Without her lover around to counsel her, she had no idea how to act otherwise. In all her life she had not ventured out of Woramni Valley, except to go to elementary school at Mamyongni just beyond the Pass, and even that trip, made daily on foot, had proved most taxing. Pang was her only key to the vast, hazardous world outside, and that key was lost, closing the door forever. Pregnancy varied from eight to ten months, even longer sometimes, she had heard. If her baby was a late-comer, with luck on her side, the month or two predating the marriage might not be noticed.

But luck was not on her side. At the end of six months she was delivered of a fully developed boy. When the infant was washed and swaddled, her husband came in, driving out everybody. In her exhaustion and stupor she had a glimpse of his bulging eyes, flared nose, clenched fists, and passed out. After sunrise she heard a bustle outside the room. A servant informed her that her husband was giving a party to the whole village to celebrate his son's birthday, barbecuing the boar he had killed the night before. His clothes got torn and bloody and his body was covered, head to foot, with scratches and cuts, but the tusked beast had the worst of it in the end.

At the party he was in the best of humor, laughed a great deal, patted the backs of his guests and bragged about his "quick" work. A lusty man like him was no respecter of premarital celibacy. The story, squaring so well with the known impetuosity of his character, was instantly credited and approved. There was no scandal. Everybody congratulated him and he grinned and swaggered in acknowledgment, but when he was alone with Yongshil, which was not frequent, he did not speak to her nor look at the child. Months passed but he didn't come to her bed.

The Land Reform Act gave the bulk of Ho's possessions to his former tenants, leaving him only a few fields in the immediate vicinity of his house. He drank in excess and became more violent, beating up people left and right. With respect to Yongshil he resorted to a strange mode of behavior. He would hug, caress, and handle her like an accomplished masseur, sexually arousing her; then at the sign of her pre-orgastic urgency, when she panted for relief, he would suddenly leave off and go to the village whores, making no secret of it. She loathed his approach, shuddered and shrank from his touch, and her senses refused to be excited, but then he was patient. He would spend the whole night, if necessary, applying his art until she showed genuine signs of arousal. The only way to be rid of him fast was therefore to work herself into a trance and develop an insensitivity to his ministrations, but after months of it she became a nervous wreck, an insomniac with muscle ache and cardiac palpitation.

Then the war came. The South Korean government got pent up in a hundred-mile perimeter of Pusan, and the North Korean People's

Army was everywhere with their upstart collaborators. Pang returned to the village, eluding the checkpoints and roadblocks set up to conscript all young men, especially college students. Pang's education had just been resumed after a year's interruption as he had to work to support himself and save for his tuition. He had reregistered for his junior year that spring.

Pang went straight to Ho's house to see Yongshil and tell her what had happened the night they were to elope. Surprised by his father while packing, he disclosed their plans. The father became furious and gave such a blow to the wayward son's head that the son passed out until the next day when he woke up with a one-way ticket to Seoul in his pocket.

At the door he was met by a precocious three-year-old boy, Sungnam Ho, whom he knew instantly to be his own son. The boy wanted to know where he had come from and what tanks and guns were like. Pang played and talked with him, quite forgetting the purpose of his visit. Suddenly, Ho's burly frame stood beside him like a wall.

"Come, weasel," growled Ho, who had never called him by his name. Pang followed mechanically to a back room through the inner courtyard.

"So you are the lover who's come home to claim

your bastard."

"I don't understand," Pang faltered.

"I have always thought that bastard's face was familiar. He certainly has none of the Ho features. The proof is right there, in your face, in your body. But I'll make one difference between you and your bastard."

With lightning speed Ho seized Pang by the throat, knocked him flat on the floor, planted his massive knee on his chest and abdomen, and tore off Pang's trousers. In one terrible moment of blinding agony, as the assailant chewed off his genitalia, all of Pang's senses went dead. When he recovered consciousness, he was at his house, attended by Yoo and his parents.

The People's Army was desperate for manpower in their increasingly costly drive to the south to run the Americans off the peninsula, and rounded up anybody, old and young, even teenagers and emaciated consumptives to fill their thinning ranks at gun point. But they let Pang be, even after his wound had closed, because by their classification, he was no man, nor woman either. Having plenty of enemies and eminently qualifying as counterrevolutionary, Ho went into hiding in the neighboring hills which he knew better than anybody.

When the UN forces recaptured Seoul, Pang

returned. The capital was in utter ruins, many parts of it still burning. Housing was nonexistent. Malnourished and diseased, people lived in makeshift sheds and huts in the charred grounds, digging in the rubble and ash, while the winter laid its early grip that year, water freezing in mid-October. As he walked along Chongno Avenue, mesmerized by the gaunt, gutted skeletons of what were elegant structures of a few months before, Pang ran into a classmate, Yongtay Jon, from Jolla Province, who asked him to come to his previous lodging house. Chungnimdong, a slum on the north side of the railroad station, was no exception to the general devastation. Jon's place was luckier than most. The rest of the house had been bombed flat but one room had survived, although there was no door or window. The holes had to be stopped with straw sacking, newspaper, or cardboard. The privy stood at the end of the property, just a hole in the ground near a half-collapsed well, which severed as the water supply for the entire neighborhood.

The one-room house had two other occupants, Kwangshik Im, a one-legged man, and Myongja Shin, an epileptic semiautistic girl related to the owners of the house. She had lived there as maid but been abandoned when the family sought safety elsewhere. Pang trudged wearily home after dark, after a day of stopping at all likely shops and offices to ask for a job, any kind of job, but there was none for him. New businesses were coming in rapidly to Myongdong, Chongno, South Gate, and other marketplaces, but they were overstaffed with their own families and relatives. He walked all over town until his legs gave under him, yet after every rebuff he renewed his search telling himself that the next stop might be just the place waiting for an eager worker like him, to give him warm food and shelter and even a scholarship for his education. Exhausted and hungry, he returned to the Chungnimdong room for a share of boiled rice and soy sauce, the bounty of his schoolmate Jon whose family sent him money from the country.

In the middle of the unheated room Kwangshik crouched under a grimy quilt. In a corner, staring blankly into space, Myongja sat without shifting her position, her cold-discolored skin showing through her tattered skirt. Jon, the keeper of this menagerie, was not home yet, tied up as he was with his English studies at an institute. As soon as Pang entered the room, Kwangshik pushed out his neck from under the quilt like a turtle, holding the edge of the blanket around his neck, and launched the usual catechism and tirade, calling him all sorts of names, pointing out the futility and presumption of his search for a job. Nobody would hire an imbecile like him. It was arrogant vanity to aspire beyond his station and desire to work his way through college, in the meantime imposing on the good nature of a friend. Instead, if he were an honorable man, he should enlist in the army, just as Kwangshik had done. Pang should join the victorious march to the north, mopping up the Communist remnants. There would be plenty of food. Any demur on Pang's part was shouted down. In his excitement Kwangshik would sit up on the mattress and lecture on the evil of advanced learning. Then, expanding on patriotism, on the beauty of the army career, he would strike the floor with his fist, wildly wave his crutch in the air, and call Pang some more names before turning to Myongja for approval.

"Isn't he an idiot, an absolute good-for-nothing parasite?"

She sat unresponding, expressionless, totally uninvolved in the altercation. Jon arrived simultaneously with the curfew siren. After watching him bunch up by the kerosene lamp to write his poems, which never got published, Kwangshik ranted on the perversion of language by poetry. Jon didn't pay attention to the criticism. Exasperated, Kwangshik snatched a sheet of paper and burned it at the lamp. Unoffended, Jon motioned him to move over and got under the blanket in his street clothes. Pang followed suit and crawled in on the other side. Myongja unrolled her own quilt and curled up in a corner.

Occasionally, the routine was varied when Myongja's father, a gentleman and scholar of the old school, came back after his peregrinations in the countryside selling India ink, brush, and other writing equipment, writing name plates, signs, charms, documents, even personal letters for unlettered people. Taking his poverty stoically, he asserted that calligraphy, as ancient as the Korean soul, could not die. When anybody showed interest in his merchandise, he was apt to give it away on credit. The turnover of his inventory was therefore rapid but he had little money to show for it. Nevertheless, he managed to drink and displayed the best of his art to the residents of the Chungnimdong room. Then, armed with some money from Jon, he left for the country again not to be heard from for days and weeks.

One day the old man Shin wrote to Jon. Kwangshik had opened the letter, being the unchallenged censor of all mail, and showed it to Pang when he came in. In a florid cursive, with an abundance of learned phraseology, the letter said that a scholar artist like Jon needed an obedient, reliable wife like Myongja, that her epilepsy was a minor defect due to no fault of hers and indeed a blessing compared to the volatility of many healthy women, that unless he heard otherwise, he would consider her married to Jon and regard him as his son-in-law.

"I approve it one hundred percent, wholeheartedly," Kwangshik shouted, waving the letter before Pang. "What do you say?"

"I don't know. It's none of my business."

"None of your business!" shrieked Kwangshik. "Is that your gratitude? This concerns your benefactor closely and is this how you show your gratitude? We have to look out for his welfare and make sure that when a good thing like this comes along, it does not slip through his fingers."

"I don't know whether Myongja will be such a good thing," Pang persisted.

"Only a saint like Jon deserves an epileptic. It is his duty, his destiny," vociferated Kwangshik, his veins rising and his fists shaking at imaginary opponents.

When Jon returned, Kwangshik pushed the letter in front of him, telling him to marry the girl right away. Jon smirked and continued writing his endless poetry. In the meantime Myongja's belly had become bigger, and daily Kwangshik badgered both his friends that Jon should marry her. Although Jon didn't seem concerned one way or another, Pang felt the incongruity and injustice of it keenly. He had no doubt that it was Kwangshik himself who had brought about Myongja's condition. To dump her off on Jon seemed wrong. Something had to be done fast about the girl. Her eyes were becoming glazed and her square face was turning sickly yellow. She had difficulty making the smallest movement. Lately Pang had been cooking their morning meals. Myongja could not get up and when Kwangshik kicked her off the bed, she went into her fit, throwing up the whites of her eyes, frothing at her mouth, her limbs shaking piteously in a fetal coil. Her fits became more frequent longer.

The UN forces had captured the North Korean capital of Pyongyang and had reached the Yalu, the Manchurian border. But there were reports of reverses and retreats, the Chinese having crossed the border, entrenching themselves with several armies. There were whispers of a full-scale retreat, all the way back to Pusan, and people were already moving out of Seoul. No word came from Mr. Shin. Pang had not found any job. Jon's university recessed early for the winter and he had to leave for his province. It was the last evening meal together. Jon had bought some cuttlefish, soy sprouts, bean curd, and other extras, leaving the rest of his monthly allowance with the three in the care of Kwangshik. From now on the three of them had to fend for themselves somehow.

"You should take the girl with you," Kwangshik said to Jon.

"But I don't have her father's permission," Jon said.

"He has not only given you permission," shouted Kwangshik, "he has given you an order to take her with you wherever you go."

Frustrated at getting nowhere with Jon, he turned to Pang.

"You are a traitor," he said.

"Why?"

"Because you do not volunteer and fight for your country. Because you are thinking of getting higher education when the country is in trouble. You have betrayed your people. I will inform the authorities of your treachery and they'll shoot you."

Kwangshik seethed and fumed and Pang rose to avoid the place, but Kwangshik grabbed him by the arm.

"Tonight I'll make you enlist in the army," he said.

He picked up the kitchen knife and cutting

board and a sheet of paper.

"Sit down and do as I tell you," Kwngshik said, pulling Pang down to the floor. "Write down in blood that you are a coward and a traitor and that you'll make amends by enlisting. I'll deliver it to the district commandant personally."

Before Pang could respond, down came the knife with a whack causing a stinging sensation to spread up his hand. The thumb had escaped but all the four fingers had been slashed off. While the wound was being dressed and the blood wiped and washed off, Kwangshik got up, supporting himself on his crutches, and left the house, hobbling in the snow. After buying alcohol and mercuro-chrome for Pang's wounds from his own allowance for the trip home, Jon left Seoul the next day.

On the east coast the US Tenth Corps, with its First Marines, got surrounded by the Chinese and barely escaped annihilation. On the west coast the Eighth US Army fought out a similar Chinese encirclement, losing nearly all its equipment and a whole division of men. Two South Korean armies got wiped out. The American troops and their allies were withdrawing faster than they had advanced. Everyone was panic-stricken. Frightening rumors of Chinese brutalities and North Korean reprisals circulated. One's very being in South Korea in the territory occupied by the UN forces was incriminating enough. Hadn't they cheered the UN forces as liberators? Everybody was sure that he would be killed as an American collaborator, as a people's enemy.

Pang took Myongja to the railroad station to board a refugee train. Snow piled inches deep on their bundles, heads and shoulders. They had to run from one track to another. Many got run over while taking a shortcut under the trains. Still people kept crawling under them, under the very cars with bodies stretched at the wheels like fish on a hook. Pulling the heavy, sickened body of Myongja after him, as well as their bundles, Pang waited and ran and waited and ran, unable to sleep. A train might leave any minute and they had to be ready, at the right spot. After being pushed around in the milling, scurrying crowd without sleep for three days and nights, he began to hallucinate. Snowflakes turned into flower petals. The bleak scenery, the screech of wheels, the yell of refugees, the cold, hunger, disease, wound, pain, and death, all turned into the harmony of a sweet spring afternoon, a fragrant hillside with newgrown grass, soft and warm to the touch. Pang woke with a start. A train, consisting of some coaches, flatbeds, and stakes, stood right before them, to which the crowd of refugees was making one big desperate dash. With Myongja in tow, Pang ran to the coaches, but it was impossible to get near the doors. At the windows, smashed open, people pulled and clawed at each other to scramble in first. The flatbeds, loaded with tanks, guns, and armored trucks, swelled up fast, like leavened dough. People fitted their bundles under and around the vehicles and weaponry, fortifying their positions with their luggage. There was a body under one flatbed, dragged a few yards, the skull crushed under the massive wheel, the brains spilling out. People paid no attention, stepped right over it and climbed on. The stake car Pang and Myongja finally managed to get near was already filled up to the brim, twelve feet high. Bundles got pitched in and people climbed on furiously. Pang had not settled one minute, squeezed between people and bags, when a woman next to him screamed. Her child had been squashed to death under the bundles. The train whistled to signal departure, and the crowd on the platform, which kept swelling, became frantic. More bundles flew in overhead and many hung on to the edge unable to climb in. People got trodden under and children got separated from their parents. Nobody heard their piercing cries. The train moved at a snail's pace with innumerable stops on the way, as the tracks got preempted by higher priority transport.

Upon reaching Pusan, Pang and Myongja were sent to a refugee camp on the nearby hills, dotted with makeshift shacks. Recorded as man and wife by the clerk who had more important things to take care of than listen to a long story, Pang and Myongja were assigned to a unit with about twenty other families. Within the shack the families made partitions as best they could with their bundles and with boards and sticks they could scrounge, making spaces enough just to fit their bodies in. The climate was warmer but the wintry rain and wind stung. The only function of the galvanized iron roof was to collect and cascade the rain water onto the sleepers. The public toilet, a hut with a trough and pit dug into the ground, overflowed. Unable to find a foothold inside, the refugees relieved themselves around the hut, in an increasingly wider radius. They had to go a mile to get water and waited in lines for hours with their buckets. The lines extended all the way to their camp. Myongja gave birth to Miyon, but died soon thereafter in one of her seizures. Her whole body had swollen to three times her normal size and one couldn't see her eyes.

Pang worked at various jobs in and around Pusan, supporting himself and Miyon, and went after the Armistice to Seoul, back to the

Chungnimdong house. Nobody claimed the house and after some rebuilding and repairs he could register it in his own name. He had to postpone his college education indefinitely in his efforts to earn enough to keep up the property and rear Miyon, who fortunately showed no sign of epilepsy. Playing with her, taking her to the doctors, to the park, preschool and kindergarten, and to special lessons whenever he could get away from work proved to be a full time job.

Then he got a letter from Woramni. Sungnam Ho, Yongshil's and Pang's son, had been left an orphan under bizarre circumstances. After the Armistice, Byongwon Ho seemed to settle down to a period of industrious husbandry, sowing and harvesting cash crops, but soon reverted to drinking and took up gambling with a passion. Nobody cared to play with him because he wouldn't stop until he or his opponent got cleaned out, generally the latter. One day a stranger showed up at the village, flaunting a bag full of new money, in crisp, ribboned 100-sheet bundles, and wanted to join the card games. He won at the minor circles and soon confronted Byongwon Ho. At the end of two days and nights of playing, the stranger took all of Ho's money. Cramming his cash winnings, seemingly carelessly, into his pockets instead of the bag, he stood up to leave.

"Sit down," Ho roared, grabbing the man's throat. "Play some more."

"Put up the money," the stranger said, undaunted.

"I stake my house and all my land against your cash."

"Not enough," the stranger said, holding up his bag.

Ho tried to borrow from the neighbors but nobody came forward. The stranger said he would humor him and play one more time if Ho would put up his wife, too. After a short consideration, Ho consented. The stranger made everybody witness it, and the game was on. Ho lost again, and looked the picture of a bomb about to explode. Cool and unruffled, the stranger rose.

"You can't leave here alive," Ho barked.

"You won't go back on your word before all these witnesses," the stranger said. "Before you do something you might regret, wait for me to bring down your wife to see what she has to say about it. I've won her fair and square, but if she still wants to hold on to the man who has thrown her off like a rotten stick, I won't take her. She is all yours. You deserve each other. In the meantime hold on to this bag. I'll come right back. I know my way."

Aiming at Ho's face, the stranger threw the bag,

which Ho caught, dodging. Ho sat, anchored down by the bag. Nobody dared to follow the stranger, who sauntered up the road nonchalantly to Ho's house. After a while the onlookers commented on the stranger's trusting nature, as they glanced enviously at the fat bag. Ho said nothing and held on tightly to the brown leather bag like a brooding hen. As the dusk of winter descended early on the mountain valley, the villagers said they had better go up to the house and see what had happened. It was certain that the stranger, accompanied or not by Yongshil, could not have slipped out of the village without passing the gambling house, situated at the mouth of the village on the way to Roof Pass. The other way out was up the back hill, past the cemetery, down into Skeleton Gulch, which led nowhere, as it was surrounded by precipices, a challenge to the alpinist even in summer and quite impassable in winter when snow piled in drifts several feet deep. Beyond these heights towered yet higher rises and peaks in the never-ending folds of the Tabak Range.

"Let's go up and see what he is doing," somebody suggested.

"Let's first open the bag up and see how much he is worth," another said.

They all thought this was an excellent idea, but

Ho merely grunted, not relaxing his hold on the bag.

"You know, fellows," somebody insinuated, "for all we know the bag may hold nothing but newspaper."

Waking up from his daze, Ho hurriedly undid the clasp, revealing what looked like 100-won bundles in mint condition.

"Count them," another skeptic stated. "I bet they are all short a few notes."

When the tie ribbons were removed, blank white sheets cut to the size of a regular note tumbled out from between the two face notes which turned out to be counterfeit on closer examination.

"Catch the swindler!" went up the outcry, as they ran toward the house. The stranger and Yongshil could be seen disappearing behind the back hill into the snow and shadows of Skeleton Gulch.

"I'll teach them both a lesson," swore Ho, grinding his teeth.

"Let's get them," the others said, who had also lost money to the stranger.

"No, you fellows stay back," Ho said. "It's my business. I'll have to tear that bitch up."

They knew better than to interfere and stayed behind, not doubting the issue between the scrawny little man and the seasoned fighter Ho. Well acquainted with the path, Ho caught up with the fugitives quickly enough and soon those below heard screams, screams of two men and a woman locked in a mortal fight. Some said perhaps they should go up before real harm should come to any of them but the consensus was to wait it out. No further sound reached them and the whole countryside was submerged under the snow falling heavier than before. Finally, the villagers went up holding torches.

At the foot of the gulch lay the body of Ho with his neck broken. There was no sign of the other two. The piling snow had erased all tracks. The search continued the next day to no avail. Early next summer they found the half skeletal bodies of a man and a woman in the third valley after the gulch. The cash on the man and the clothes of the woman identified them as the gambler and Yongshil.

Pang brought Sungnam to Seoul and sent him through school. Miyon promised to be a good scholar but soon got involved in the English club at her high school with its American advisors, GI's who wanted to mix with the local population. She then dropped out of school altogether and didn't even come home at night. After much inquiry Pang found her living with an American Sergeant at Yongsan. Before he could do anything about it, they had moved to another address and by the time he caught up again, the GI had been transferred to Honolulu and Miyon went with him. Pang concentrated on Sungnam's education but in his second year in college he went to the army and came out a few years later a motiveless, disillusioned dropout, who vented his resentment against society by harassing and baiting Pang for an explanation of their close resemblance. Then the American Consulate told Pang that papers were ready for him to apply for a passport and visa to come and live with his daughter in Honolulu.

•   •   •

"Why do you want your no good son to come over?"

"Because he is my blood. I won't know peace until he comes here and feels what it is like to live in a free country, without fear and humiliation."

"But he will never be your son. The law will not recognize the relationship. Adoption is no good because he is too old."

"There must be ways. I have saved up over $10,000 here. Besides, we have the house in Seoul and the property in Woramni."

A thought occurred to me.

"He can marry a citizen," I said. "Why not marry Miyon? She's been married and divorced too many times to let a thing like that bother her. That way you get to keep everything in the family, the money and the people."

"But they are like brother and sister."

"They have no blood or legal relationship."

"Won't I have to explain?"

"No. Probably they suspect as much anyhow. Just tell her she has to. Say it is your last wish or whatever. Surely she owes you that much. My only worry is whether he will be able to adjust to the fast pace of American life once he gets here."

"He will. He will become a new man. He can't help it."

I listened without comment, recalling the growing statistics of Korean immigrants on the welfare roll.

Muriel walked in to point out that I should perhaps drive Pang home, unless he was going to sleep downstairs. He rose guiltily, and insisted on walking home, but I pushed him into my car. When I returned and went to bed, Muriel wanted to know what we had talked about so long.

"Oh, nothing. Just about the Korean War, the usual stuff, you know, the debacle, the recapture, the retreat...."

"Good night," she said, uninterested. A US-born citizen married to someone born in Korea, she had heard enough about the war, perhaps too much from too many, me included.